Printed in the United States of America

Published by MARLvision Publishing

Sarasota, FL

ISBN: 978-0-9833763-1-6

ACKNOWLEDGEMENTS

Without the constant love and support of my wife Marcee and our beautiful children, I could not begin to accomplish the things I do. My family is everything to me. I love them more than a few simple words can express.

TABLE OF CONTENTS

ONE

Faith was not a big action town. Very little ever went on, unless you counted the cattle auction every Saturday at noon, or square dancing every Saturday evening, which Dalton Connors never participated in.

Dalton spent most of his time working. He wrote best-selling paperback westerns at the rate of two a year. His finances were in good shape. There were a couple of people in town he spoke to regularly. Other than that, he kept pretty much to himself.

It was Friday morning when the world changed. Dalton didn't realize at the time it was the whole world, but it didn't take long to figure out as much.

He was on his front porch, smoking a cigarette and drinking a cup of coffee, taking in the crisp morning air. Cotton ball clouds hung against a pale blue sky. The sun was just up and already starting to warm the day. A hawk soared overhead. This was one of Dalton's small pleasures in life—early mornings in Faith, Wyoming.

He couldn't be sure whether he felt or heard it first, but he was suddenly aware something was coming. A high-pitched squeal shattered the early-morning tranquility at about the same time a dark object flew over Dalton's house, leaving thick gray smoke in its wake. It traveled north to south. Dalton tracked its descent until it slammed into the ground about a half a mile away.

Dalton was in the process of watching black smoke rise when his telephone rang. He went inside, crossed through the living room, and entered his office to answer the old rotary dial phone on his desk.

"Did ya see that thing, Dalton?"

It was Jed Cotts, Dalton's best friend. Jed was somewhere in his seventies, though he never gave specifics.

"It went right over the house," Dalton said.

"Whattaya think it was?" Jed asked.

"A meteor maybe," Dalton said. "Landed about half mile south of here."

"How 'bout we drive out and have a look see," Jed said, nearly bursting with excitement.

"I've got some work to finish up," Dalton said. "Tell you what, though, I'll meet you at Edna's in an hour. We'll grab some coffee and head that way."

"Sounds good," Jed said.

"See you then."

Dalton sat down at his desk and turned his attention to the old Remington he'd written all of his novels on. It was still going strong. He saw no need to fix something that wasn't broken. Using a computer might make his job easier, but he'd miss the sound of the Remington's keys clacking away in the heat of a writing streak. That noise was so much a part of the process for him that he couldn't separate it.

He was a simple man by nature. He didn't want to read his books on an electronic reader, he didn't carry a cell phone, and he wasn't going to write on a computer.

He started typing what would be his twentieth novel in a decade. Westerns were still popular. Dalton was thankful for that. His tales of gunfighters, dance hall girls, and Native American warriors had brought him a good living; he was thirty-five and financially comfortable.

Not that money mattered to him. The satisfaction came with the work. Money was a by-product. What mattered to Dalton more than anything was that he'd achieved success on his own terms. When his agent had pushed him to write something in the horror genre, Dalton had stuck to his guns and written westerns. Horror had never been his thing; he would have been a flop at it.

Dalton lit a cigarette and tried to concentrate on his latest chapter, but he couldn't get the meteor out of his mind, if the thing that crashed outside of town *was* a meteor. He had no reason to believe it was anything else, and couldn't imagine what else it could be even if he tried.

He decided to forget about work and head to Edna's. Jed would already be there anyway, and the sooner he got there, the sooner they could drive out and take a look at the crash site.

Edna's Country Café was the type of small-town place where you could get all the coffee refills you wanted for the price of one fifty-cent cup. The owner was actually a woman named Edna—Edna Jean Abernathy, to be exact—and the food was prepared from recipes handed down in her family through generations.

Edna's Country Café was also the sort of place where almost everybody in town gathered to hear, and spread, the latest gossip and news. Today the place was buzzing with talk that mostly centered on the thing that had crashed just south of town.

Henry, a regular at Edna's, sat at the counter wearing the same wrinkled business suit he always wore. Ed, a contrast in his worn coveralls, sat beside Henry. The two of them were busy chewing each other's ears off. Dalton had a guess what they were talking about, and he could only imagine how far fetched the theories had gotten by now.

The place was jumping with other customers as well. Joe Ruben, Edna's longtime cook and good friend, set two heaping plates of eggs and bacon under a heat lamp; Abigail Holden grabbed the plates and headed to the dining area.

"Hi, Dalton," she said as she passed him by.

"Hey, Abby," he responded.

He stopped long enough to watch her deliver the food, not realizing until several seconds had gone by that he was staring. He glanced around the cafe to make sure no one had noticed. Before moving on, he caught a snippet of the conversation Henry and Ed were having.

"I saw it with my own eyes," Henry said. "Came right outta the sky, big as a truck."

"Damndest thing I ever heard," Ed replied. "Whattaya make of it?"

"Flyin' saucer is my best guess," Henry said with confidence.

Dalton bypassed the two of them and took a stool at the far end of the counter.

Abby tended to Henry and Ed. "You two are something else," she said.

"Can I get some more coffee," Henry asked. "With extra sugar, sugar," he added, chuckling at his own joke, nearly patting himself on the back at his own cleverness.

"Sure," she said, rolling her eyes.

"Take it you don't believe somethin' strange landed out there in the field," Henry said to Abigail.

"Oh, no, I believe something landed out there," Abby said. "That's all everybody's been talking about this morning. I just think yours is the best explanation for what it is I've heard yet."

"Well, I think he's right on the money," Ed chimed in. "I think we got us a real UFO experience right here in Faith."

Dalton couldn't resist a smile. "And I bet there's little green men plotting on us right now," he said.

The bell over the entrance jingled in time to prevent Henry from a quick response. Jed wandered into the café wearing his customary baggy, faded jeans and red and black checkered shirt. Despite being in his seventies, he walked at a brisk pace, with no sign of wearing out any time soon.

Edna grabbed the coffee pot and headed to the end of the counter, turning up a coffee cup for both Dalton and Jed.

Jed sat beside Dalton.

"What do you know about that spaceship, Jed," Henry asked before Jed had a chance to say hello to Dalton.

"I don't know nothin' about no spaceship," Jed answered, barely glancing at Henry. "A meteor, maybe, but it ain't no spaceship."

"Meteor, my ass," Ed said. "A spaceship is what it was, I don't care what anybody has to say about it."

9

"I think you two best stay away from the home brew, that's my take on it," Jed shot back, reaching for his just-poured coffee. "Dalton says—"

"There you go with that Dalton-says nonsense again," Henry cut in. "Just because he's a writer don't mean he knows all there is to know about everything."

"I never said he knows all there is to know," Jed said. "He knows a damn lot more than you two igits is all I'm sayin'."

Henry and Ed were suitably offended by the remark and, for lack of a good comeback, went back to entertaining each other.

Dalton sipped his coffee as if the conversation hadn't occurred. The last thing Jed needed was for Dalton to come to his defense. The old man could handle himself. Dalton wasn't about to offend him by cutting in.

Outside the diner, Sheriff Colbrook's squad car went by with its lights flashing.

* * *

Sheriff Jeff Colbrook was in his thirties, with lean, chiseled features. He was usually an easy-going man with a smile for everybody, but today his face was set in a grimace.

He reached for the mic on his dash and keyed it. "Sarah, you got anything yet?" he asked.

A blast of static issued from the radio, followed by Sarah's voice. "Nothing yet, Sheriff."

Sarah was the only radio dispatcher with the Sheriff's Office. She put in as many hours as she could, not so much because she needed the money or the Sheriff's Office needed a dispatcher, but because it gave her plenty of opportunity to be around Jeff Colbrook.

"You hear anything at all, let me know, will you?"

"Ten-four, Sheriff," she responded.

Colbrook hung up the mic and continued heading toward the site of the crash. He wasn't sure what was happening yet, but he'd received a military call shortly after the crash. The call had been ambiguous at best, with someone claiming to be a high-ranking official warning him to disregard the crash until further notice. He'd waited as long as he could for further notice to arrive and had decided against waiting any longer. Whatever was sitting outside his town, Jeff Colbrook took it as his duty to investigate.

* * *

"You want some French toast, Dalton," Edna asked.

"I believe I do," he said. "Lots of bacon too, real crispy."

"Comin' right up," Edna Jean said.

She warmed Jed's and Dalton's coffees, then headed for the kitchen, shouting, "Order of French toast, Joe, double bacon, make it real hot."

"Those fellas just bite me the wrong way," Jed said to Dalton. "Flyin' saucers, if that don't beat all."

"It's to be expected," Dalton said. "Gives 'em something to talk about."

"I reckon so . . . hey, how's that new book comin' along? You bringin' back that gunslinger from the last one?"

"I just might be," Dalton replied.

"You'll save me a copy?"

"Signed, same as always."

* * *

The sheriff's patrol car slid to a stop near the perimeter of a massive smoking hole. Colbrook got out of the car and heard a hissing noise immediately, followed by the heavy THU-WHUMP, THU-WHUMP, distant at first, then gaining in volume until the hissing sound was completely obliterated by two Blackhawk helicopters appearing over the ridge beyond the crash site. The two helicopters hovered overhead and set down a couple hundred yards away.

The first man out was Colonel Clayton Edgewater. The man was in his fifties, right around 210 pounds, and about 6' 2" tall. His eyes were cobalt blue and striking as hell. There was no doubt he was here to run the show.

"You in charge here?" he called to Sheriff Colbrook, raising his voice so he was heard over the helicopters.

"I am," Colbrook answered.

"Not anymore," Edgewater said. "I'm the big chief now. Colonel Clayton Edgewater, son, and you are smack dab in the middle of a military operation."

"What's going on here?" Colbrook asked, ignoring Edgewater and looking beyond him, to where a group of soldiers formed a perimeter around the hole.

"Did you hear me, son?" Edgewater said. "This is a military operation. You will be on a need-to-know basis, and right now you don't need to know jack shit. Am I making myself clear?"

"I beg to differ," Colbrook said. "Faith is my town, and while that thing is sitting outside of my town, I need to know what the hell's going on."

"This ain't a pissin' contest, boy," Edgewater said, clearly annoyed. "The military takes priority. That means we piss further by default. And as long as we're on the subject of your quaint little town, let me inform you that we'll be setting up base camp here and coming and going as we please, without interference from anyone. Is that clear?"

Sheriff Colbrook had an overwhelming desire to knock Edgewater on his ass, but he knew better. He was in no position to fight with the military.

"It's clear for now," Colbrook said, and left it at that.

* * *

"You coming to the house?" Dalton asked, standing up and taking out his wallet.

He and Jed had decided to put off going to the crash site until later. As much as Dalton wanted to get a look, he was concerned about all the military activity in the area. If his guess was right, it would be impossible to get close this early on. Odds would improve when the dust settled.

"I think I'll stick around and see what comes of all this," Jed said. "Might wander out this afternoon, if that's all right. Maybe we can try to sneak a peek at the site then."

Dalton laid money on the counter. "Good enough," he said. "Your coffee's paid for."

"'Preciate it, Dalton."

"Not a problem."

Dalton headed for the door as Abby came out of the kitchen. "See you around, Dalton," she called after him.

He turned for a simple wave goodbye. That's all it was; that's all it should have been.

Why, then, did he feel those damn butterflies in the pit of his stomach?

THREE

The whole city was going haywire and Johnny Boscoe was right in the middle of it. Fighting, screaming, looting, gunshots, cops on foot trying to control the crowd as squad cars pushed through the pandemonium . . . it was apocalyptic chaos at its fucking best.

Johnny, with his hair slicked back, wearing an expensive Italian suit, stepped out of the coffee shop and realized this was no place he wanted to be. He was making plans to get the hell out when a skinny kid bolted past him, nearly knocking him on his ass.

"Watch where the fuck you're goin', you little punk," Johnny called after the kid.

He fished a Sobranie Black Russian from his suit pocket and lit it. The world could fall apart all around him, but there was still time for a good smoke. In fact, if the world was falling apart, Johnny was going to finish his pack.

He started down the sidewalk, shoving people out of his way as he went. He passed one storefront after another, some in flames, others simply laid open for the wild-eyed looters of New York City. It never ceased to amaze Johnny how fucking savage society was when you got right down to it. Animals in clothes.

He turned into an alley and stopped long enough to get his bearings. Maybe if he had some idea why the city had suddenly gone mad, he'd know what the hell his next move should be, but he couldn't figure it out. The situation was like a scene from one of those end-of-the-world movies. He'd heard some explosions, then the chaos had started. As far as he knew, the third world war had finally started. That's the best he could come up with. Nothing else could account for the craziness. What else could account for this madness?

He needed to get away from the city. Maybe it was less crazy somewhere else. He needed a set of wheels. At a time like this, getting a set of wheels would be a breeze.

He moved down the alley and came out in another rush of people. Across the street was a parking lot. There'd be a car there. It didn't have to be the lap of luxury. He'd take the first vehicle he could hot wire, then he'd be on his way, somewhere without the insanity.

* * *

Wanda Kowalski stumbled past a burning, demolished building. A large rock of some sort sat right in the middle of the rubble. Wanda stopped long enough to stare at the object in disbelief, then she continued on her way.

She looked a mess. Her low-cut blouse and skirt were soaked with blood, her fishnet stockings were torn, and her long brown (which looked black because of all the soot) hair was drenched with sweat. To make matters worse, she could hardly see where she was going through all the smoke in the air, which left her eyes burning and watering.

She rounded a corner and came to a complete stop as a wall of people rushed toward her. They didn't stop. She felt them smashing into her as they ran by. It crossed her mind they must be running from something, but instead of turning to follow the crowd, she pushed on. What was ahead of her couldn't be worse than what she'd left behind.

* * *

Johnny shoved his way through the crowd of people who were fighting each other over boxes of food, radios, TVs, and whatever else they could get their fucking hands on.

"Christ, it's World War fuckin' Three and you motherfuckers are killin' each other," he said, hurling people aside as he made a beeline for the parking lot across the street.

He had his sights set on a silver Grand Marquis. That would do the trick. He got lucky and found the door unlocked on the driver's side. He slid into the car, fiddled with some wires, and had the engine purring in no time. All he had to do now was get the fuck out of town, and if that meant running a few people over to do it, you could damn well bet that's what he'd do.

He turned right at the end of the street, screeching tires on the pavement. A produce truck backed out of a side street, right in front of him. Johnny cut the steering wheel hard to the left to avoid hitting the truck. The end of the car fish tailed. He cut the steering wheel the other way, straightening the car out again, then he punched the gas, whipping around the truck and thinking he was home free.

That's when the chick ran out in front of him. Instead of running her over like he'd planned to do to anybody who got in his way, he slammed on the brakes, stopping just inches from spreading her all over the pavement.

"Son of a bitch," he said.

Before he could take off again, Wanda came to the passenger side of the car and jerked the door open, sliding into the car before Johnny could stop her.

"Let's go," she said, breathing hard.

"What the fuck . . ."

"Drive, will ya?" she said.

Johnny hesitated a moment, thinking he should shove her right back out the way she'd come, then shrugged and said, "Just don't be fuckin' cryin' and shit, you got that? I don't need no chick bawlin' on my shoulder."

He jammed his foot on the gas pedal. The car's tires screamed against the pavement. The momentum threw Wanda backward, against the seat. She was about to complain, but Johnny shot her a look that stopped her in her tracks.

A Blackhawk roared overhead, flying so low to the ground that Johnny and Wanda both felt the car shake.

"What's happening?" Wanda asked, the tone of her voice a little too whiny for Johnny's taste.

"I don't have a clue," Johnny said. "Do I look like the fuckin' eyewitness news?

He glanced in the rearview mirror and saw helicopters setting down right on the streets of the city. Military trucks, jeeps, and armored vehicles were converging on New York, dropping soldiers with weapons readied for combat. Johnny may not have known what was happening, but he knew whatever it was, things were going to be drastically different after today.

FOUR

I just don't like it," Jed said. He and Dalton were sitting on Dalton's front porch, drinking beer and watching a line of military vehicles move along Route 73, heading toward the crash site. "Military vehicles rollin' into town just don't sit well with me. The military gets involved, there's bound to be a snake in the grass somewhere."

"I'd be inclined to agree with you," Dalton responded. "Doesn't seem they'd be interested if there wasn't something they wanted to keep from us, does it?"

"It's more than a meteorite, I'll tell ya that. When's the last time the military got this worked up over a hunk of rock?"

Dalton lit a cigarette and took a thoughtful pull. "Still not ready to buy the spaceship theory, though," he said.

"I ain't sayin' it's a spaceship, but somethin's goin' on those military boys got a hankerin' for, that's for sure."

* * *

Henry and Ed were eating lunch at Edna's. They hadn't moved from the stools they'd occupied at breakfast. The conversation hadn't changed much either. The only perceptible difference was the addition of a couple of BLTs. The two of them looked up with mild interest when Sheriff Colbrook entered the cafe, then turned their attention back to lunch and the topic of conversation for the day.

"Hi, Sheriff," Abigail said from behind the counter. "You hungry?"

Colbrook took a stool at the end of the counter. "Don't have much of an appetite, Abby," he said. "Coffee'll do."

Before Abby could reach for the coffee pot, a disturbance from outside drew everybody's attention. A couple of military trucks and jeeps came to a stop outside the front of the cafe. Colonel Edgewater climbed out of the lead jeep, a cigar stuck in his mouth. He stood for a moment and looked up and down Main Street, then he cleared the distance between the convoy and the entrance of the cafe in a few strides.

Henry and Ed looked star struck. They could only stare at the colonel in stunned silence. Abigail did the same. Colbrook glanced at the man without much interest, then said to Abby, "Can I get that coffee?"

"Oh, sure, sorry," she said, filling his cup.

Edgewater strode past Henry and Ed without so much as a glance. He took the stool next to Colbrook and turned up his own coffee cup, signaling for Abigail to fill him up.

"Can I get you—" she began.

"That'll be all," Edgewater said curtly.

She filled his cup and hurried off.

"We'll be setting up a perimeter," Edgewater said to Colbrook, not bothering to look at him as he spoke. "No one will come or go without my say so. I'll expect full cooperation from you and your deputies, without any complaint."

"We'll do what we can not to step on your military toes," Colbrook said.

Edgewater faced the sheriff then. "Are you getting wise with me? I've got a job to do here, and one way or the other, with or without your cooperation, that job is going to get done." He paused long enough to take a sip of his coffee. "I can see you don't like me much, and that's okay, I'm not here to make friends. You *will*, however, respect me, and you *will* cooperate with the United States Military in whatever way is required. Are we clear on that?"

Colbrook didn't bother to look at Edgewater. The man irritated him to no end, so much so that he almost did something he never did; he almost lost his temper. What stopped him was the certain knowledge it would lead to nothing good. He clenched and unclenched his fists a couple of times, bit back his anger, and said, "We're clear."

"Good," Edgewater said, the harshness of his tone lessening when he realized the sheriff wasn't going to pursue the matter. "That's real good."

Edgewater turned back to his coffee.

* * *

"You got another of these?" Jed asked, holding up an empty bottle of Corona.

"I believe I just might," Dalton said.

"Mind if I have me another? I sure do like these Mexican beers."

"I don't mind at all," Dalton said. "In fact, I have a feeling we might need a couple more before this day's passed us by."

Dalton stood and stared at the southern horizon to take in the sight of the military hoopla taking place at the crash site.

"Yep, a real to-do, ain't it," Jed said.

"Sure looks like it," Dalton agreed.

FIVE

"**S**on of a bitch," Johnny muttered.

Wanda was scrunched down in the seat, her bare feet on the dashboard. As focused as Johnny was on the traffic and getting as far away from the city as he could get, he couldn't help but notice the smooth skin and firm calf muscles of Wanda's legs. The girl was in shape, there was no denying that.

"You got a cigarette?" she asked, catching Johnny staring at her.

"Yeah, sure," he said, not the least bit embarrassed at being caught.

He reached into his jacket pocket and pulled out a pack of cigarettes, tossing them onto the dash so Wanda had to lean up to get them.

"You got a light?" she asked.

He looked over at her and shook his head. "You want me to fuckin' smoke it too?"

He took out a lighter and tossed it to her.

"This fuckin' traffic," he complained, turning his attention back to the vehicles lined up in front of him.

"What's goin' on?" Wanda asked.

"I look like an encyclopedia to you?"

"Jeez, what crawled up your ass?"

"You crawled up my ass," he said.

"You tried to run me over."

"You ran out in front of the fuckin' car."

Johnny saw an opening in the traffic and jammed his foot on the gas, cutting off a vehicle in the lane next to him as he moved into the right-hand lane and made a few hundred yards before he had to step on the brake again.

"So, what's your story?" he said, glancing over at Wanda. "Besides the fact that you're a whore, I mean."

"Fuck off," she shot back.

"What? You ain't a whore? Gimme a fuckin' break, and don't be so sensitive."

"A girl does what she's gotta do," Wanda said. "That don't make me a whore."

Johnny shrugged. "I'm not judgin'. I was just makin' an observation."

He saw another opening and went for it, squealing tires as he cut across traffic and exited the highway to an orchestra of honking horns.

They found themselves in a run-down neighborhood that looked as if it hadn't been populated in some time. There were hardly any cars in sight that looked like they'd run, and the brick tenements lining both sides of the street looked empty, with doors and windows standing open or busted.

"Nice neighborhood," Johnny muttered.

"Yeah," Wanda agreed. "Look, maybe we should get back on the highway."

"We need to find a place to stay 'til the traffic dies down," he said. "I'm gonna kill somebody if we stay on the fuckin' road."

He turned at the end of the block and drove until a Super 8 came into view. He veered into the parking lot and shut off the car.

"You comin' with me?" he asked, his hand resting on the door handle.

"What else have I got to do," Wanda said, shrugging.

They walked to the office together. A fat woman with greasy hair and glasses sat in an overstuffed, bug-infested chair behind the counter. She was big enough to dwarf the chair. She stuffed her face with pizza slices and flipped through a tattered copy of *Cosmopolitan*.

"I'm payin' for one bed," Johnny said to Wanda. "You can sleep with me or on the floor. It doesn't make any difference to me."

"Well, aren't you just Prince Charming," she responded.

22

"It ain't like you've never slept with a strange guy, now, is it?"

The fat clerk looked up with mild interest, wiping a thick strand of cheese from her mouth. "What can I do for you two lovebirds?"

"We need a room for the night," Johnny said, taking out his wallet and laying a one-hundred dollar bill on the counter.

The fat clerk struggled to raise herself from the chair. The beached whale was practically stuck, and Johnny almost laughed.

She finally managed to break free. She took his money, made change, and slid a key across the counter. "Room thirty-one, second floor. Sheets are clean."

"I sure hope so," Johnny said.

The room turned out not to be as bad as Johnny expected.

Wanda fell back on the bed, spreading her arms out like wings as she let out a relieved sigh.

A siren screamed by outside. Johnny went to the window, parted the curtains, and took a peek. He could see their car from the room, which made him feel better.

He turned away from the window, lit a cigarette, and said, "We gotta find out what the fuck's goin' on out there."

He turned on the TV. A blonde newscaster was on, staring at the studio camera with a professional smile and a twinkle in her eye.

". . . authorities refuse to comment any further, but it appears in many parts of the country the military has taken control . . ." the blonde newscaster reported as a series of live shots of military vehicles and soldiers flashed across the TV screen.

"Are you seein' this shit?" Johnny said.

Wanda was still lying back on the bed, oblivious to the news report.

The blonde newscaster came on again. "It seems a number of meteorites have struck across the country, but many wonder why the military has assumed such a strong position . . ."

23

Johnny changed the channel until he came to a black newscaster doing his best to look good while he maintained an appropriately grave expression. "More reports are coming in by the minute," the newscaster said, "detailing more acts of violence . . ."

Wanda had propped herself on her elbows to stare at the TV. Her eyes were wide and her skin had taken on a pale tone as the reality of the situation began to take effect.

"This is fuckin' crazy," Johnny said.

He switched channels again. A veteran newscaster in his 50s, with a fake tan and wrinkles his numerous surgeries couldn't hide, was reporting the news as casually as he'd talk about the weather. "We have reports that police agencies throughout the country are working under military command at this time, and there have been talks of a nationwide curfew, though it's unclear . . ."

"I ain't gonna be under no fuckin' curfew," Johnny said, glancing at Wanda and doing a double take when he saw how rough she looked. "You look like hell," he said.

"Thanks," she said. "Got another cigarette?"

She kicked off her heels and extended a long, shapely leg. Johnny lit two cigarettes as he watched her roll her torn stockings down. Wanda caught him staring but made no attempt to scold him, so he didn't bother looking away. He was sure she played it up for his benefit. When the stockings were gone, he dragged a chair over beside the bed and straddled it backward, facing Wanda and handing her one of the cigarettes.

"You never gave me an answer," he said. "What's your story?"

"Besides being a whore, you mean?"

"Hey, I didn't mean it bad, ya know. I've just been around the block a few times. I know things." He took a long pull on his cigarette and blew smoke at the ceiling. "My name's Johnny, by the way. What's yours?"

"Cheri," Wanda answered.

Johnny frowned. "I look like I was born yesterday?"

24

"Wanda, okay? It's Wanda Kowalski. Not flashy enough for the street, so I go by Cheri. You got a last name, Johnny?"

"Boscoe," he said.

"Well, Johnny Boscoe, I know a few things too." She looked him over. "I know you're a guy in a five-hundred dollar suit who hasn't made it to the top of the ladder yet."

"I'm on my way, honey," Johnny came back defensively. "At least, I was before all this shit hit the fan. God knows what the fuck I'm doin' now."

Wanda smiled at him. It was the kind of playful, seductive smile that told a guy like Johnny he might get lucky. Never slow on the uptake, he said, "It looks like we're gonna be together for a while. How do we pass the time?"

Wanda stood and peeled off her top, uncovering pale breasts with hard pink nipples. Johnny smiled for the first time since waking up that morning, because for the first time since waking up, he saw something he recognized.

"That's as good a way as any," he said.

He stood, kicked the chair aside, and took Wanda in his arms, kissing her hotly as he guided her down on the bed.

SIX

The street outside Edna's was crowded with military vehicles and soldiers standing around smoking, their M-16s slung over their shoulders. Inside the diner, the locals were gone. The once-quiet diner had become home and headquarters to the military. Abigail was doing her best to take orders and deliver food. Edna Jean was doing the same, while Joe worked the grill as fast as he could, flipping burgers with one hand and dropping orders of fries and onion rings with the other.

Abigail grabbed two orders from beneath the heat lamp as Joe replaced them with two more. She carried the food to a corner table, passing a heavyset soldier who waved and said, "Can I get another Coke over here?"

Sheriff Colbrook entered the diner. He stood and looked around, frowning at what he saw.

"Be with you in a minute, Sheriff," Abby said, rushing by him on her way to deliver an order.

"Take your time," he said.

He headed for a clear place to stand at the end of the counter. Edna brought a pot of coffee over. The sheriff held a hand up, palm out. "None for me, thanks," he said. "Looks like business is booming."

Edna's face was creased and worn. "I could do without it. What can I get for ya, Jeff?""

"A cheeseburger with the works is fine," he said. "No rush on it."

"If I can feed all these animals," she said, indicating the crowd with a jerk of her thumb, "I can damn sure feed you."

Edna went off to fill his order and Abigail came breezing in behind the counter.

"You taken care of, Sheriff?" she asked.

"I'm good, Abby, thanks."

A chorus of angry voices rose outside as two soldiers began shoving each another. Sheriff Colbrook looked but showed no interest in breaking up the fight. They could all kill each other for all he cared.

"Ya know, Abby, maybe I could use a coffee after all," he said.

She smiled. "Comin' right up."

* * *

A cloud of dust kicked up behind Dalton's truck as he swung onto the dirt road heading toward the crash site. Jed sat beside him. Ahead of them were three military cargo trucks and six armed soldiers.

"You better slow down some," Jed said. "Those fellas don't look too friendly."

"They'll get over it," Dalton replied.

He didn't bother slowing down until he was a few hundred yards from the roadblock. By that time, the soldiers were moving into a defensive position. Dalton eased his foot onto the brake and came to a stop. One of the soldiers came around to his side of the truck.

"How you doing?" Dalton asked, waving and giving the soldier a big, friendly smile.

"Only authorized personnel beyond this point, sir," the soldier responded. His features were set in stone. Dalton's friendly demeanor was wasted on him.

"Just came to see what all the commotion's about," Dalton said, not about to give up so easily. He knew full well the odds of making any headway were nonexistent, but he hadn't driven all the way out here to turn around without making at least some effort.

"I can appreciate that, sir, but this is as far as I can allow you to go," the soldier told him, glancing at the other soldiers for support before returning his attention to Dalton.

Dalton looked at the roadblock and back to the soldier. "Must be some kind of big deal, huh?" he asked. "I mean, all this military . . ."

The soldier's knuckles tightened around his M-16. The other soldiers fanned out around Dalton's truck Three took up post on the passenger side. Jed watched them move into place. He tapped Dalton on the arm without taking his eyes off the soldiers on his side of the truck. "I don't know, Dalton, these boys don't look to be in the mood for chat."

"Sir, I'll have to ask you to turn this vehicle around and leave the area," the soldier on Dalton's side of the truck said. "If you don't do so immediately, I will be forced—"

"No need for all that," Dalton said. "I'll turn around."

He threw the truck in reverse and backed up, then turned around and went back the way he'd come. A glance in the rearview showed the soldiers moving back to their original positions. Like it or not, there was no way anybody would be getting close to the crash site. Whatever was going on beyond that perimeter, the military had it locked down and off limits.

* * *

The compound set up around the crash site was bustling with activity. Military trucks and jeeps rolled from one end to the other, delivering soldiers and information from one post to the next. The crash site itself was located directly in the center of the compound and measured about a quarter mile in diameter. Two scientists in protective gear were in the hole, examining what appeared to be a large meteorite oozing a viscous black substance. Parts of the giant rock pulsated and undulated as if it were alive.

Not far from the hole, a jeep skidded to a stop and Colonel Edgewater climbed out of the passenger side, making a beeline for the two scientists examining the rock. A soldier standing beside the hole offered a salute. Edgewater saluted back and leaned over to look into the hole. "Should my men be wearing protective gear?" he called down.

The two scientists looked up at him. One spoke up, his voice muffled through the covering over his head. "I can't say for certain, sir. We have yet to determine the make-up of the object. Before we can—"

"Is it still leaking shit?" Edgewater cut in.

"With all due respect, sir, does it appear to be leaking to you?" the scientist asked.

Edgewater's face reddened and his temples began to throb. One of the many things he couldn't stand was a smart ass. He could smell a smart ass a mile away, and this guy in his protective gear, jerking his dick while he played with a rock, was a smart ass.

"Fuck the due-respect shit," Edgewater said. "Just because you're part of some special scientific unit doesn't mean you come in here with your bullshit attitude, you understand what I'm saying? Does your college degree catch my drift?" He was on a roll now and not about to stop. "It's your job to find out what that fucking thing is. It's my job to control the goddamned situation while you do that. In the process of doing my job, I will ask any fucking question I damn well want to ask, and I *will* get a straight answer. I'll do whatever *I* deem necessary to ensure the safety of my men. Now, is there anything I've said here that you don't understand?"

"I understand you just fine, sir, but keep in mind that we are not under your command, and as you pointed out, we have our job to do. Now, if you'll excuse me, I'd like to get back to it."

Edgewater exploded. "You son of a—"

"Colonel, sir, General Claymont on the horn," the driver of Edgewater's jeep called out, just in time to prevent an explosion that would have left an unfortunate scientist with his head torn off and up his ass.

Edgewater glanced at Private Daybrook holding up the receiver, then down at the two scientists again. "You idiots keep me posted of all developments," he said, then he turned and headed for his communication with the general.

SEVEN

Johnny and Wanda were lying in bed, tangled together in the sheets and smoking cigarettes. She sat up, allowing the sheet to slip away from her breasts. Johnny reached over and stroked one of her nipples.

"Save some energy for later," she said.

"I never run out of energy, baby," he said, grinning as he continued to play with her nipple.

"Where are we going to go?" she asked.

"Not a fuckin' clue. You saw the news. The whole country's goin' crazy. The fuckin' army, curfews, that's some serious shit."

Car tires squealed outside the motel room, drawing Johnny's attention to the window. He looked back at Wanda, who was staring at him like a lost puppy dog. Her chin was propped in her hand. That was the kind of gaze Johnny didn't want to see. It meant she was going all mushy on him, and that was something he couldn't afford in his life.

"You're a big, strong guy, aren't ya?" she said. "You'll take care of me."

"Look, I ain't no fuckin' hero," he told her. "I take care of myself. You wanna tag along, that's fine by me, just don't go expectin' too much."

She smiled at him. "I think you might surprise me, Johnny," she said. "Might even surprise yourself."

"Don't bet on it."

"I am betting on it," she said. "I mean, you come off like a real jerk, but I think there might be more to you than even you know."

"I think you might be wrong about that."

She plucked the cigarette from between his fingers and leaned over to put her cigarette and his out in the ashtray on the night table, then she faced him again. "We'll just have to wait and see about that, won't we?"

"I guess we will."

She slid the sheet away from him and reached out to stroke his semi-erect cock, which responded to her touch immediately.

"I told ya I never run out of energy," he said.

"I can live with that," she said, climbing on top of him.

"What makes you think you're gonna get the chance to make a decision like that?" he asked, cupping her bottom as she settled down on him.

"Because I think you like me," she replied.

She wiggled her bottom invitingly.

"Is that right?"

"Yeah, that's right."

He pulled her face to his and kissed her hard on the mouth. She kissed him back, thrusting her tongue deep into his mouth as she began to ride him. He tangled his fingers in her hair and returned her enthusiasm. It wasn't long before they reached a climax together, collapsing again in a sweaty heap.

For the first time in his life, and certainly for the first time since this whole crazy thing had begun, Johnny felt like maybe he'd found someone he could keep around.

EIGHT

The scientists were still examining the oozing black rock when Edgewater approached the hole again. He'd just gotten off the radio with the general and it was time he put these two dumb asses in their proper place.

"Okay, dick heads, listen up," he called down into the hole. "The game has just changed. I'm in charge of this fuck-off operation now. That tasty tidbit of trivia came straight from the Pentagon. I say shit, you damn well better drop your fucking trousers and ask me what pretty color I'd like. Are we clear on that?"

The scientists were annoyed, but they seemed to understand not to push the issue, which satisfied Edgewater to no end. "I want a prelim on this big motherfucker within the hour," he said. "Answers, boys, that's what I want. I want some fucking answers."

"Yes, sir," one of the scientists responded, with no indication in the tone of his voice that he was anything other than exasperated.

Edgewater started to turn away, but a hissing noise from inside the hole brought him around again. The rock began to steam and liquefy. The scientists' muffled screams tore through the steam as they scrambled to get out of the hole.

* * *

An old pickup truck rolled to a stop outside the crash site perimeter as two soldiers flanked it. Henry was behind the steering wheel and Ed was in the passenger seat.

"What landed out here?" Henry demanded, leaning out his window.

"You'll have to turn around and go back the way you came," the soldier on Henry's side of the truck stated flatly. "Only authorized personnel beyond this point."

"I ain't beyond the point, now am I?" Henry said. "I'm right outside where I ain't supposed to be, which puts me exactly where I should be. That about right?"

"Sir, I'll ask you one more time to turn your vehicle around and leave," the soldier said. "After that, we'll have to take you into custody."

"Sounds more like a direct command than asking," Henry said. He looked over at Ed. "What do you think?"

"Sure sounds like we're being told to me. Nothing polite about it either."

The soldier on Ed's side of the truck spoke up. "You are in direct violation of—"

Henry cut him off. "I served my country in the military, so don't go giving me any speeches. I fought in a world war before you boys were even in diapers, which I'd lay dollars to doughnuts is more than you two can lay claim to. Now, I live just a few miles down the road here, and all I'm askin' is whether or not somethin' from another planet has landed damn near in my backyard?"

"And I'll say it for the final time, this is military business—"

An explosion shook the ground. Both soldiers spun to look toward the inside of the perimeter where it seemed like all hell was beginning to break loose. That's when Henry made a decision that he might have taken back if he'd gotten the chance. He opened his door and got out to get a better look.

The truck's door was rusty and squeaked loud enough to be heard over the chaos inside the perimeter. The two soldiers spun quickly in Henry's direction, bringing their M-16s up to open fire. A hail of bullets tore into Henry's chest and riddled the windshield of the truck. Inside the truck, Ed had no time to duck. His head disintegrated, painting the interior of the truck with vibrant shades of red.

* * *

Edgewater drew his .45 and looked down into the hole. Black liquid bubbled up around the scientists, making any rescue attempt pointless. He turned to where a small group of soldiers had fanned out with their weapons ready.

"I want a full alert issued," Edgewater said. "I want every son of a bitch in my command armed and ready for combat."

The soldiers all nodded and moved out, issuing commands as they went. Edgewater took one more look into the hole and shook his head.

"Guess neither of you will be shittin' anytime soon," he said.

* * *

A kid on a bike left the sidewalk on the corner of First and Main, rolling across the street without looking. The kid always looked before he crossed, but his attention was focused on the black cloud rising into the sky south of town.

The driver of the Acura didn't see the boy. He was too occupied with the same black cloud as the kid. The front of the Acura slammed into the boy on the bicycle. The boy flew off his bike and landed several yards away. His bike went under the car, twisting and tearing apart as the Acura's tires squealed against the pavement.

The driver of the car got out and ran straight for the kid, yelling for help as he went. Edna and a few customers came outside to see what the commotion was about. Edna went back inside to phone the sheriff.

Colbrook arrived five minutes later. The driver of the car was kneeling beside the boy, still in a state of panic.

"I didn't see him, Sheriff," the driver said. "He ran right out in front of me."

"Take it easy," Colbrook said. "Step back and let me have a look."

Colbrook helped the driver to his feet and moved him back a few steps, then he knelt beside the boy and checked his pulse. There was nothing there. Not even the slightest beat of a heart. The kid was gone.

Colbrook stood up and turned to deliver the news to the driver. He was about to open his mouth when the boy's hand twitched just slightly and then darted out, grabbing Colbrook's ankle.

"Jesus Christ," the driver screamed, stumbling backward, thinking only that he had to get away from what he was looking at.

The kid's eyes were wide open and he was drooling. It didn't seem possible, but that's exactly the way it was.

The kid was also doing his best to drag the sheriff down, but Colbrook managed to jerk his foot away. The kid lunged again, snapping at Colbrook's ankle like a rabid dog.

Colbrook kicked the kid in the head and backed away, his hand moving to his holster.

The boy tried standing on legs that were shattered and bent. When his legs wouldn't support him, he dragged himself toward the sheriff, snapping and snarling.

"What the hell's wrong with him?" the driver of the car screamed, no longer worried about what he may have done to the kid.

"Besides the fact that he's dead?" Colbrook said, drawing his revolver.

"You're going to shoot the kid?" the driver squawked.

Colbrook answered the question by raising his gun and firing. The bullet struck the boy in the shoulder and jerked him sideways, but it didn't stop him. Colbrook fired two more rounds, both bullets striking the kid in his upper body.

"Holy mother of God," the driver said.

This time Colbrook aimed more carefully. He squeezed off a round that hit the boy between his eyes, exploding his head in a shower of blood and bone fragments. What was left over fell to the ground and stayed down.

* * *

"Shoot it," one of the soldiers who'd shot Henry and Ed yelled.

The two soldiers opened fire on Henry, who had gotten up shortly after being shot the first time around. Their bullets plastered his chest, ripping through flesh and bone, but Henry kept coming.

"The head," one of the soldiers yelled. "Shoot the son of a bitch in the head."

35

The soldiers adjusted their aim and opened fire again, exploding Henry's head like a ripe watermelon. Henry stood headless for a couple of seconds before dropping.

"Did you see that shit?" one of the soldiers asked. "Fucker was walking around with no head and his guts hanging out."

"I got eyes," the other soldier said.

They circled around the truck to take a look at Ed, who was missing half his head. Blood and jelly-like brain matter dribbled from the opening.

"It's the head. I was right," the first soldier said. "That's why this one stayed down. He's already missing half his fucking head."

The second soldier put a short burst of 5.56 mm slugs into what was left of Ed's head. "Just to be on the safe side," he said.

* * *

Edgewater stood directing operations with his back to the crater. He didn't see the two scientists crawling from the black muck minus the protective suits. Most of what was left of their skin hung in tiny strips and flaps over bone.

Private Jacobs came to a skidding halt in front of the colonel. "Colonel, sir, I advise that you take a look behind you," he said.

Edgewater was agitated with the interruption, but he turned anyway, and saw the two skeletons coming his way. "What in *the fuck* am I looking at?" he said.

"It looks like a couple of skeletons, sir," Private Jacobs responded. "I mean, if I were to make a guess, sir."

"I know a goddamned skeleton when I see one, private," Edgewater declared.

Two more soldiers joined Private Jacobs, speechless by the sight of the skeletons almost on top of Edgewater now. Edgewater glanced at the approaching skeletons with mild annoyance, then he stepped aside. "Blow the sons of whores away," he instructed his men.

Private Jacobs and the other two soldiers opened fire all at once. Bullets ripped through the skeletons, throwing bone chips in every direction, but the damn things kept coming.

"Aww, Jesus," Edgewater mumbled when the soldiers ceased firing.

He drew his Desert Eagle and fired one shot at each skeleton, shattering their skulls in turn. The soldiers stood dumbfounded as the sacks of bones collapsed almost at Edgewater's feet.

"You dumb fucks never saw *Night of the Living Dead?*" Edgewater said, holstering his Desert Eagle. "Now get a goddamned flamethrower over here and toast those fuckers."

* * *

Edna's Country Café was packed with soldiers. The volume level was intense to the point of being mind numbing as the soldiers all spoke louder in an effort to out-talk each other.

Abigail and Edna were behind the counter, having caught up with orders long enough to take a short breather.

"Why don't you go home, little one," Edna said. "I can handle this."

"There's no way I'm leaving you here by yourself," Abigail said.

"Don't you worry about it. I can handle everything just fine, and there's always Joe if I need him. Besides, I may lock up early, whether these army boys like it or not."

Abigail hesitated, then said, "You'll call if you need me?"

"Of course I will," Edna said. "Won't need to, though. Go on home and rest."

Abigail untied her apron and handed it to Edna. "Thank you," she said.

"You're welcome" Edna said.

Abby called bye to Joe and made her way through the crowded diner. She couldn't get out the door fast enough. Once she was in her car, she took a deep breath and slowly exhaled, relishing the silence. She turned the key in the ignition. The engine almost turned over, then sputtered out. She turned the key again. This time there was nothing more than a click.

"Damnit," she said. She popped the hood to take a look at the engine, not that it would do her much good. She didn't know anything about cars.

An army truck rolled by while she was looking under the hood. "Hey, baby, need a jump?" a soldier called out from the back of the truck, which was followed by a series of cat calls.

"How 'bout a hot wire," another called out.

Abigail turned away from the truck, ignoring the soldiers as she took another look under the hood. As the army truck made a left at the end of Main Street, Dalton's Dodge Ram came into view at the opposite end of the street. Abigail looked up in time to see him pull into the parking space beside her.

"Need a hand?" he asked through the open passenger window.

"I'd love one," she said, relieved to have him there, not only to help with her car, but because she'd feel better having him around if the army truck came back by.

"Let's see what I can do," Dalton said, coming around the front of his truck to look under the hood of Abby's car. He fiddled with a few wires. "Have to admit, I'm not much good with mechanical things," he said, grinning sheepishly. "I *can* give you a lift somewhere, though."

"I was on my way home," she said.

"I'll take you home, then I'll call Frank's Motors. How's that sound?"

"I'd appreciate that," she said.

* * *

Edgewater sat at the counter in Edna's diner, eating a thick burger and wiping grease from his chin with the back of his hand. He washed every couple of bites down with a gulp of iced tea. His movements were mechanical. Eating to him wasn't something to be enjoyed. Food was fuel, pure and simple, and taking time to eat it for pleasure was out of the question.

Edna came around behind the counter to grab two more plates from under the heat lamp. She was exhausted. "Surprised Henry and Ed haven't been back in," she said to Joe, making conversation she didn't really have time to make.

Edgewater took note of the comment.

Edna delivered the two orders. There were three more waiting when she came back. Before she could pick anything

38

up, Edgewater pushed his empty tea glass across the counter. "I need a refill on the tea," he said.

Edna grabbed a tea pitcher without missing a beat. She began filling his glass.

"Your friends are dead," he told her with a certain amount of cruel pleasure.

"Excuse me?" Edna asked.

"The two yokels you mentioned earlier . . . dead. Got themselves in the way of a military operation."

"You talkin' about Henry and Ed?"

"If that was their names, that's who I'm talking about. They got a little crazy out at the site. My men had to shoot them."

His tone was as relaxed and matter of fact as if he were discussing a story on the news. Edna's face had gone white.

"You're sure about this?" she asked, setting the tea pitcher aside.

"I'm always sure about what I say," Edgewater told her. "That's a guarantee."

Edna turned away from the counter, no longer concerned with Edgewater or his crass behavior.

"I could use an order of fries to go with my tea," Edgewater said.

Edna didn't hear him. She forgot about the orders waiting to be delivered. All she could think about was the way things in the world had suddenly turned upside down.

"Joe," she called out, heading to the kitchen. "I think I'm going to need a break."

* * *

Abigail's trailer was small and plain. She and Dalton sat at a little table in the kitchen, enjoying some iced tea. Had Abigail been able to step outside her body and look at the two of them from an outsider's perspective, she would have seen the wide-eyed look of complete adoration in the way she watched Dalton as he talked. She couldn't see the look on her face, but she knew it was there nonetheless. She knew how she felt about Dalton Connors—had known for quite some time—she was simply waiting for him to figure out how he felt about her.

39

She'd asked Dalton what he thought might be going on in town, with the military moving in the way they had. In truth, she was tired of talking about the military and whatever it was that had landed, but if she could keep Dalton around, so much the better.

"I'm not sure," he said. "I know the military doesn't throw a party like this unless there's a good reason."

"I wish they would leave," Abby said. "They make me uncomfortable." She blushed then. "Does that make me a bad person?"

"Why would you ask a thing like that?"

"I mean, they're our military. They protect our country."

"Doesn't make all of them good," Dalton said. "They're people, Abby, just like you and me. Some are good, some are bad."

"They seem mostly bad to me, and that colonel, he thinks he's God."

"I don't much like him myself," Dalton told her, "but I guess he's just doing his job."

"I wouldn't want his job," she said.

"I wouldn't want it either," he agreed.

* * *

Sheriff Colbrook and two of his deputies, Ken Hagerman and Billy Swanson, were engaged in serious conversation. Sarah was at her desk, listening to what was being said.

"I don't give a damn what Edgewater has to say about it, I want to know everything that goes on," Colbrook said.

"I understand," Hagerman agreed. "They come stompin' through our town, barkin' orders. . . . The whole damn town's on edge."

"And it should be," Swanson said. "We got a dead kid that wouldn't stay dead. What about that wouldn't put a town on edge?"

The phone rang and Sarah answered it. "Sheriff, it's for you," she said. "It's Edna. She sounds real upset."

Colbrook took the phone. "What is it, Edna?"

40

Hagerman, Swanson, and Sarah saw the color drain from his face.

"What's wrong?" Sarah asked when he hung up.

"Henry and Ed," he said. "Seems our All-American boys killed 'em."

* * *

Colbrook got out of his car and headed for the perimeter of the crash site, dead set on answers. He didn't care if Edgewater and the entire United States Military stood in his way. Hagerman and Swanson's car was parked at an angle behind Colbrook's car. They followed on his heels, pushing to keep up with him as he approached two armed soldiers standing guard. One of the soldiers stepped in front of Colbrook.

"That's as far as you go, sir," he said.

"We're here to investigate the deaths of two men," Colbrook said. "I'm going to need access to this area."

"I'm sorry, but this is as far as I can let you go," the soldier said.

"You listen to me . . ."

A jeep inside the perimeter approached at high speed, its horn blaring as it came to a sliding halt beside the sheriff. Edgewater was in the passenger seat, looking as if someone had just disturbed a healthy visit to the shitter.

"What in the hell is going on here?" he asked.

One soldier started to speak, but Colbrook cut him off. "I'm here to find out what happened to the two men who were killed here."

"It's a simple matter," Edgewater said. "They were told to leave the premises. They didn't comply, so my men shot them."

"Your men murdered two people because they wouldn't leave when you asked them to?"

Edgewater's temple throbbed. "Let's get something straight here, Barney Fife. This is a military operation set in motion by the President of the United States of America. I do not owe you any explanation or justification for anything I, or anyone under my command do, nor will I attempt to give you any."

41

Edgewater took a cigar and a camouflage Zippo from his pocket. He lit the cigar and considered the situation a moment, then he said, "What I will do, since I'm an all-around nice guy, is educate you." He motioned his soldiers to stand down. "Leave your tag-alongs here and come with me."

Inside the compound, Edgewater led the sheriff to a large tent surrounded by armed soldiers. With one hand on the tent flap, Edgewater said, "What you're about to see is going to put the smack dab on your small-town ass, Fife. You hear me?"

Edgewater entered the tent and stood aside for Colbrook to follow. The tent was set up for medical operations, with steel tables and an array of surgical tools lying everywhere. A kid in military uniform was huddled in one corner of the tent, chained to a stake hammered deep in the ground. Part of his face was gone, leaving bloody bone exposed. There was a hole in his stomach, and some of what he had on the inside was now on the outside.

"That used to be Private Willie Sparks. He's dead now," Edgewater said. He paused for effect, then said, "What the hell am I talkin' about," he added, sounding like a real corn-stalk hick. "Have I lost my ever-lovin' mind?" The country accent was his personal dig at the sheriff and his small community. He paused again, hoping his private joke hit home. When it didn't, he continued, this time dropping the Hoosier accent. "Dumb shit got some of the black goo on him. You *don't* want the black goo on you. Understand what I'm saying?"

"No, I don't understand," Colbrook said, trying to take it all in. "Lay it on the line without being an asshole about it."

Edgewater grinned around his fat cigar. "This is your lucky day, son," he said. "I'm feeling generous. Matter of fact, I'm feeling real un-asshole like, so I'm going to let you in on a little secret. How would that be?"

NINE

Johnny and Wanda were asleep in a tangle of motel sheets. Three gun shots rang out, ripping through the silence of the night. Johnny bolted up and gathered his clothes from the floor, throwing his clothes on as he covered the distance to the window.

The sound of squealing tires added to the chaos outside. Something was happening, and it didn't sound like something Johnny wanted to be any part of.

Wanda was slower to respond. She sat up, still groggy, rubbing her eyes with the backs of her hands. "What is it, Johnny?" she asked.

Johnny pushed the curtain aside and peeked out the window in time to see a car speeding out of the motel parking lot. "Get dressed," he told her. "Something bad just went down out there."

"What?"

"I don't know yet. Put your clothes on. We're gettin' the hell out of Dodge."

Wanda, wearing only panties, swung her feet to the floor and reached down to gather her clothes. Johnny opened the door and stepped outside. There were three cars in the parking lot besides the one he and Wanda had come in. The office door was standing open.

Wanda came up behind Johnny, still wearing nothing but her panties.

"Looks like somebody robbed the office," Johnny told her.

"Better take a look," Wanda said.

"Why should I go look? It ain't my business, and besides, there's nothin' I can do about it if somebody hit the joint."

"You could at least make sure nobody's hurt," she said, again with that whiny voice that usually bothered him, but now didn't seem quite so bad.

He hesitated, took another look at the open office, and said, "All right, if it'll make you feel better, I'll look, then we get the fuck outta here. You get your clothes on and be ready."

He made his way to the office, stopping several times to look around. The night seemed preternaturally silent. The kind of silence that made a man worry.

There was nobody behind the front desk. The cash register was open. Johnny leaned over the counter to get a better look . . .

The fat clerk rose up from behind the counter. Three bullet holes dotted the front of her shirt, which was soaked through with blood and clinging to her massive boobs. Pink bubbles of spit foamed out of her mouth and ran down her chin in thick strands, hanging like snot from a runny nose.

Johnny backpedaled in time to avoid the fat clerk's arms as she groped for him. He stumbled and almost fell before he managed to turn himself away from the slobbering behemoth. He hit the door at a full-out run, making it back to the room in half the time it took him to get to the office.

Wanda was standing outside the room, smoking a cigarette, when Johnny jerked the car door open.

"Get in," he yelled.

Johnny was already fumbling with the ignition wires when Wanda slid into the passenger seat. She was about to ask him why he was in such a hurry when she caught sight of the fat clerk lumbering toward the car.

"What's her problem?" she said, oblivious to the clerk's present unfortunate condition.

Johnny glanced up and saw the clerk coming. "She's got three bullet holes in her chest for starters," he said, then went back to work on the car.

The fat clerk was only a few feet away by the time the car's engine fired up. Johnny slammed the car in reverse as the fat clerk lunged. No way he would have imagined she could throw that weight around, but she cleared the distance to the vehicle like it was nothing. Her bulk clipped the front of the car as Johnny backed out of the parking space. She hit the ground and rose up again, redirecting her lumbering bulk to chase after Johnny and Wanda as their car squealed away.

Johnny thought they were home free as they screamed out of the parking lot. A truck appeared from nowhere, narrowly missing them. Wanda gripped the dashboard and screamed so loud Johnny cringed.

He glanced in the rearview and saw the fat clerk still coming. Not fast, but she was giving it all she had.

"This is the fuckin' Twilight Zone," he said.

Johnny swung a left at the first intersection, leaned on the steering wheel to swing the ass end of the car back into place, and was about to take a deep breath when he saw an accident at the end of the street. Johnny recognized one of the cars as the one he'd seen speeding from the motel parking lot. There was already one police cruiser on the scene, with sirens wailing in the distance.

"Fuck me," he said.

He slammed into reverse and mashed his foot down hard on the gas. The sound of metal against metal was deafening. Johnny took one look in the rearview mirror and groaned.

"This shit can't get any worse," he said.

Then he found out how wrong he was.

The windshield of the police cruiser was shattered. The cop was sprawled against the seat. His head was twisted at an angle Johnny knew it shouldn't have been twisted in, and what was left of the cop's face was a conglomeration of bloody skin and bits of the windshield.

"This ain't good," he mumbled.

To make matters worse, the front of the police cruiser was attached to the back side of Johnny's car, making it impossible for Johnny to drive away.

"Johnny . . ." Wanda called out.

She was leaning out of the car, pointing in the direction of the accident. Johnny looked to see what had her panties in such a bunch. More police cruisers were arriving on the scene, along with an ambulance.

Two men were fighting; another man climbed out of the wreckage to join in the scuffle.

Somebody screamed.

Johnny hurried to pull Wanda out of the car. "The cop's dead and we're stuck to his fuckin' car. We're gonna have to beat feet . . . your head's bleeding. You okay?"

"I think so."

He took her hand and they started across the street, while gunshots began to erupt in the vicinity of the accident.

They were well away from the chaos by the time the dead cop in the cruiser decided to walk again.

TEN

Dalton heard the crunch of gravel as a car pulled into the driveway. He'd been sitting on the front porch, thinking to himself how things had gone to hell so fast. The car approaching was Sheriff Colbrook's. Dalton stood and leaned on the railing as he watched Colbrook get out of the car.

"You got a minute, Dalton" the sheriff asked.

"I do," Dalton said. "You want a beer?"

"I'd normally say no while I'm on duty, but I'm not inclined to turn down the offer at this time."

Colbrook followed Dalton into the house. Dalton took two beers from the refrigerator and joined the sheriff at the table. He could see the man had aged a great deal since the arrival of the military. The lines on his face were somehow deeper, and there were dark spots under his eyes.

"This about Ed and Henry?" Dalton asked.

"It's a damn shame what happened there, and it pissed me off to no end. I confronted Edgewater about it, but it gets much worse than Ed and Henry dying, if you can believe that. Edgewater showed me something disturbing."

"Disturbing?"

"Dead things coming back . . ."

"You want to repeat that."

"Dead things, Dalton. It's the goddamned rock. There's some kind of black substance, I don't know. It kills you and then brings you back."

Dalton didn't respond. He didn't know how to respond. What the sheriff was talking about was something out of a horror movie, made up by some Hollywood writer with an imagination. Dead things didn't come back.

47

"You think I've lost my mind, I know" Colbrook said. "I saw it two times today. The Parker kid was hit by a car and deader than a nail. He got up and came after me. Out at the site, a soldier chained up, drooling at the mouth, just as dead as the kid. It's happening all over the world, Dalton. This ain't just a local thing. What's happening here is happening everywhere, and while I'm no fan of Edgewater, he's the least of our problems."

Dalton shook his head slowly, took a long pull from his beer, and said, "What the hell is the military doing about it? And how did the kid you're talking about get affected by the rock? Was he even near the crash site?"

"Don't think he was," Colbrook said. "Edgewater says it can affect you if it touches you, but you can breathe it too. Problem is, the black stuff is alive. It travels. They're trying to contain it, but it goes in the ground, gets into the water, travels through the air. . . . They don't know how far it's gotten, Dalton. Any of us could get hit with this thing, and since it's everywhere, there's nowhere to run."

Dalton thought about this a moment longer, then said, "There anything we can do besides wait to get infected?"

Colbrook had no answer for him.

* * *

Deputies Heck Johnson and Brady Walker were standing in a well kept cemetery just outside of the Faith city limits proper. The headstones were mostly old in the section the deputies were in, with some dating back as far as the early 1800s. Despite the fact that neither Johnson or Walker really believed what the sheriff had discussed with them, being surrounded by so many grave stones was still disconcerting.

"I think Colbrook's lost his mind if you want my opinion," Walker said.

"I don't want your opinion," Johnson shot back. "What I want is for us to get this job done so we can get out of here."

With that, Johnson shined his flashlight over a row of headstones, casting shadows that looked like figures moving through the darkness.

"This whole thing is creepy," Walker said. "Dead things walking. That's about the stupidest thing I've heard yet."

"It came straight from Colbrook, and he got it straight from the military," Johnson said. "I don't much believe it myself, but Sheriff Colbrook ain't prone to overreacting. There's gotta be something to it."

"I don't believe a goddamned word the military says. I think they've fucked something up and don't want us to know about it." Walker stopped and took a hanky from his back pocket, dabbing at his forehead. "I'd rather be home with a cold one right now. That's what I need. A nice cold one."

"Let's just do the rounds and we can go," Johnson said. "You keep flapping your jaws and we'll be here all night."

A twig snapped somewhere nearby. The deputies spun in different directions, shining their flashlights around the cemetery in an attempt to pinpoint the source of the noise.

"Probably just an animal," Walker said.

"Yeah, probably," Johnson agreed, wanting badly to believe it.

Walker took a deep breath and took another step. He was just about to add something to the conversation when he stepped into an open grave, screaming until he hit bottom and had the wind knocked out of him.

Johnson leaned over and shined his light into the grave. Walker was flat on his back on top of a coffin. Walker's own light had slithered away from him and he was groping for it, which meant he wasn't seriously injured, or at least didn't appear to be much worse for wear.

"Gimme a goddamn hand," he said.

Johnson tucked his flashlight under one arm and grabbed hold of Walker's hand, giving him a hard tug. Walker half-climbed as Johnson pulled him, finally making it over the lip of the grave. He straightened and began brushing dirt from his pants.

"Jesus, I can't believe they leave those things open like that," he said.

He looked up at Johnson, his eyes widening when he looked over Johnson's shoulder. Johnson saw the look on Walker's face and spun around, following Walker's line of sight. The deputies brought their lights up at about the same time, illuminating a staggering corpse.

"Holy shit . . ." Walker said.

The thing was in the early stages of decay, with skin beginning to fall away from its face and hands. Its lips were almost gone; thick strands of black ooze hung from its chin.

Johnson went for his gun. The corpse lunged. Johnson side stepped and spun to track the zombie, bringing his gun up in a two-handed grip. The corpse collided with Walker, who was still standing by the open grave, and both Walker and the corpse went tumbling in.

Johnson leaned over the edge of the grave, trying to draw a bead on the corpse, but his flashlight was on the ground somewhere behind him, and without it, he could hardly see a damn thing.

"Get him off me," Walker called up. "Get the fucking thing off me!"

"I don't wanna shoot you," Johnson said.

The next time Walker opened his mouth, it was to release a scream that chilled Johnson's blood. What Johnson didn't see was that the corpse had taken a nasty chunk out of Walker's neck. He didn't see the corpse eating Walker's face either, but he didn't need to see anything to know his friend was gone.

He fired three shots into the open grave, took a deep breath, then fired three more shots. He listened. Nothing moved. Not the dead thing, which was finally dead again, and not Walker, who had suffered a fate Johnson didn't even want to imagine.

"Aw, jeez, Brady . . . I'm sorry," he muttered, standing up and holstering his weapon. "Damnit, I—"

He never had a chance to finish his thoughts. A dead woman shambled from the darkness behind him and flung herself onto his back, wrapping her twig-thin arms around Johnson. Her bony fingers covered his face; he could smell the stench of her decay filling his nostrils.

50

He tried to shake her off, but she hung on like some rodeo corpse. There were others too, rising from their graves and slipping from the shadows. The bony bitch sank her teeth into Johnson's shoulder and jerked her head back, tearing away his uniform and bringing a chunk of bloody meat with it.

Something without legs dragged itself up and started gnawing on Johnson's ankle, and another corpse went to work on his left leg, biting down hard, pulling away tendon and muscle in strips.

Johnson fumbled for his gun. There weren't enough bullets to kill the rotting corpses, but he could make it better on himself. There was no way he was going down like this. He'd blow his fucking brains out, and wouldn't that serve the motherfuckers right. He wasn't coming back a corpse.

Before he could get the gun to his head, one of the dead things swiped it from his grip. After that, everything went black.

* * *

"You heard from Heck and Brady," Sheriff Colbrook asked Sarah, who was manning her post at the radio.

"Not yet," she said. "I'll keep trying."

Colbrook lit a cigarette.

"I thought you quit," Sarah said.

"We're in the middle of a zombie apocalypse. Smoke 'em if you got 'em."

Sarah smiled. She'd never smoked a cigarette a day in her life, but if there was ever reason to start, this was it.

"Send Ken to the cemetery to round those two up," Colbrook said.

"Will do, Sheriff," Sarah replied.

Her hand was almost on the transmitter when an explosion rocked the building, startling her. The sheriff was already halfway to the door. Sarah forgot all about Ken and followed the sheriff outside.

Thick smoke rose into the sky over the crash site as a second explosion came, sending a massive ball of flame skyward.

At Edna's, soldiers began pouring into the streets and rushing into their vehicles. Colbrook and Sarah could hear the frantic commands being issued as the military vehicles pulled away, heading for the crash site.

"Looks like all hell's breaking loose," Sarah said.

"You might be right about that," Colbrook agreed.

* * *

The twisted, flaming remains of two Blackhawks lay on the ground inside the perimeter of the military compound. Several makeshift buildings were raging infernos, and the smoking remains of a Humvee sat in the center of the compound.

Dead soldiers littered the ground and their living counterparts ran over their corpses. Sporadic gunfire erupted over screams and shouts. It was chaos at its best, and Edgewater stood in the middle of it all, his Desert Eagle in hand. If he didn't take charge soon, this whole goddamned operation was going to Hell in a handbasket.

"Contain this goddamned situation," he yelled above the chaos, stalking across the open field toward the downed helicopters.

A burning soldier stumbled from the wreckage of one of the Blackhawks, so far beyond pain he wasn't even screaming. He stumbled to Edgewater, falling to the ground within a few feet of him.

"For your own good," Edgewater said. He aimed his Desert Eagle at the burning soldier's head and squeezed the trigger, putting a hole in the soldier's head that threw off bits of flaming tissue and bone fragment.

Edgewater could see it was all over here. The compound was all but gone. There were corpses rising everywhere—good men gone dead. He began to put them down again, one by one, as calmly as he could. No honorable soldier should be walking around dead, and Edgewater considered it his goddamned duty to blow their heads off.

He raised his voice and stated in as loud a voice as he could, as if anyone cared to listen, "Sleep tight, fellas, and don't let the zombies bite."

He continued blowing corpses away as he worked toward the nearest jeep. There was no point hanging around now. The balance of power was shifting and the odds weren't in favor of the living.

* * *

Sheriff Colbrook slowed his cruiser when he saw the military vehicles approaching from the direction of the compound. He hit the lights on top of his unit and angled his car to block the approach of the convoy. The lead vehicle crawled to a stop, with the other vehicles following suit.

Colbrook got out and approached the lead vehicle.

"What happened up there?"

"Lost control of the base, sir," the driver said.

"Where's Edgewater?"

"I wouldn't know, sir. Please move your vehicle so we can proceed."

Colbrook returned to his car and allowed the convoy to pass. Now that the compound was lost, he knew his town was about to become a madhouse, and the military was going to be the least of the problem.

ELEVEN

Johnny grinned as he put some weight on the gas of the Corvette. "Now this is what I'm talkin' about," he said, looking over at Wanda.

"Keep your eyes on the road, would ya?" she said.

"I got it covered, baby. Just relax and enjoy the ride."

She lit a cigarette and rolled her window down. "I'm hungry."

"We gotta stop for gas. You can get somethin' then."

He whipped over into the slow lane and backed off the pedal as he exited the highway. There was a tiny diner and trailer park on one side of the road and a Phillips 66 on the other. He pulled into the gas station.

"Don't go in without me," he told Wanda.

He stuck the gas nozzle into the tank and flipped the lever on the pump. Nothing happened. "Looks like I gotta go in to get the gas started. Let's go."

Wanda got out of the car. They crossed the parking lot and entered the gas station, which looked like a tornado had blown through. The shelves were overturned. Food and soda cans were scattered all over the place.

"Grab somethin' to eat," Johnny said. "I'll get the pump—"

A teenage kid with blank eyes and wearing a bloody Phillips 66 shirt rose from behind the counter.

"That kid don't look so hot," Johnny said. "Grab somethin' and let's go."

Wanda didn't grab anything. She ran for the door, with Johnny following right behind her. The zombie gas attendant climbed over the counter and went after them.

Johnny and Wanda hightailed it back to the car. The zombie kid was moving faster than a dead kid should be moving. Johnny started the car and wheeled away from the gas pump.

The gas nozzle came out of the tank and slammed into the zombie. Johnny did a U-turn and barreled down on the kid, hitting him head on and flipping him up and over the Corvette.

Johnny turned the car around for another pass.

"Come on, Johnny, let's go," Wanda said.

"Fuck that." Johnny replied. He drove over the kid, splitting his head like a ripe melon. "Now we can go."

* * *

Not more than two miles from where Johnny and Wanda encountered the lumbering kid at the Phillips 66 station, Eddie was having an encounter of his own. He was supposed to have been working at the Phillips 66 with his buddy tonight, but he had the chance to screw Sue Ann, and he wasn't about to pass up the opportunity.

"What was that?" Sue Ann said.

She was lying half naked beneath Eddie. He ignored her and tugged her panties down. Before she could make any more objections, he unhooked the clasp of her bra, pulling the satiny cups away to bare her tits.

"Eddie," she whined. "somebody's out there. They could be watching."

He cocked his head and listened. "Just the wind," he said, then he was inside her, pumping his way to a toe-curling climax.

Sue Ann lay motionless as he fucked her. The sooner he got his rocks off, the sooner they could get out of this stinking barn. Whether Eddie believed her or not, she'd heard someone out there. Probably some sheep-fucking country boy . . .

"Eddie . . ."

"Yeah, baby, say my name," he grunted.

"Eddie . . ."

"Louder . . ."

She started screaming then, twisting and squirming beneath him as she pounded his back with her fists.

"Oooo, a wildcat," Eddie groaned.

Sue Ann clawed at his back, leaving deep red trenches.

"Behind you," she screamed.

55

Eddie wasn't looking anywhere. His eyes were closed and he was on his way to Hollywood.

"Here goes, baby," he said, groaning as he spent himself inside her.

Sue Ann brought her knee up, driving it into his balls. A flash of white-hot pain tore through Eddie, the likes of which he'd never felt before. He rolled away from Sue Ann, clutching his damaged nuts.

Sue Ann grabbed him by the shoulders and shook him. "Not now, Eddie, not now," she pleaded. "Don't pass out on me."

He tried to shake off the pain.

"Get up!" she screamed. "They're coming."

"What the fuck . . . ?" he muttered, still clutching his balls.

He was halfway up when he saw what had Sue Ann so freaked out.

"Those things are fuckin' dead," he said.

He gagged at the stench of rotting flesh and moldy clothes as the dead things started crowding into the barn like a bunch of cattle. Two of them were ahead of the pack and nearly on top of Sue Ann and him. Eddie grabbed a nearby pitchfork and jabbed at the corpses.

"They're pretty fuckin' slow," he said. "If we make a run for it . . ."

He was set to do just that when Sue Ann screamed. She grabbed at his arm, which made it hard for him to use the pitchfork. He swatted at Sue Ann and said, "You crazy fuckin' bitch."

She grabbed at him again, this time dragging him to his knees. He tried to push her away, but she had a death grip on him and wasn't letting go.

The corpses moved in.

Eddie shoved Sue Ann hard, finally getting her away from him. She fell back against the wall hard enough that her head bounced off the wood, and Eddie actually heard what sounded like her skull cracking. He felt bad, but he wasn't going to die here because she was in a panic.

He started jabbing the pitchfork at the nearest zombie—a rotting thing with bits of gray flesh dangling and eye sockets crawling with maggots.

Eddie rammed the pitchfork through the zombie's neck, severing its head. One down and too many to go. They were multiplying and spreading out. Some of them had made their way around Eddie and were all over Sue Ann. He wasn't sure she was still alive, and even if she was, there was no way he'd be able to help her now.

He saw an opening and ran like hell, swinging the pitchfork at anything that got in his path. He was almost out the door when he heard Sue Ann call for him, and she sounded so goddamned desperate.

He almost went back for her, changed his mind and started for the exit again, then decided to go back for her after all.

"Shit," he said, disgusted he was even considering such a dumb move.

He charged in, screaming like a wild man. His knuckles were white around the wooden handle of the pitchfork as he brought it down on top of the pile of dead meat covering Sue Ann. He speared them and tossed them aside, digging his way through the heap of rotten flesh until he reached Sue Ann. "Come on," he said, grabbing her by the wrist and pulling her to her feet.

It was too late by then to go out through the front of the barn. A lumbering horde of rotted flesh blocked the exit and was closing in on them. The only way out was up a rickety ladder and through the hay loft. From there, they could jump to the ground and run for the car.

Eddie sent Sue Ann up the ladder first. When she was in the loft, Eddie stuck the pitchfork in the nearest corpse and left it there. He climbed the ladder, then kicked it away when he was in the loft, not sure if the dead things could climb, but too smart to leave it to chance.

They were in luck. There was a conveyer belt in place for moving hay. Eddie crawled over to the opening and looked outside. There were only a couple of corpses outside the barn.

"We can do this," he told Sue Ann, who was huddled against the wall. "Don't get freaky on me now, you hear me?"

He helped her on the conveyor belt. She took one look outside and froze. Eddie hadn't risked his neck for her so they could die now. He threw her over his right shoulder, then he climbed onto the conveyor belt and started down. His knees buckled under the stress about halfway down. He lost his balance and tumbled head over heels the rest of the way.

The car was about a hundred yards away. The zombies in the barn had begun drifting back outside. Eddie pulled Sue Ann to her feet and ran toward the car, dragging her with him.

Thank God he never locked his doors. He opened the driver's side and pushed Sue Ann into the car ahead of him, then he slid in behind her, shoving her out of his way. The keys were still in the ignition. He grinned as he pumped the gas and cranked the engine. When Betsy fired up on the first try, Eddie broke into a fit of hysterical laughter.

"We're outta here," he said.

Sue Ann didn't look well at all. She had cuts and scratches and bites all over her body. She leaned back against the seat and closed her eyes.

"Jesus, Sue Ann, you look like shit," Eddie said. "You're gonna be all right, though."

"Thank you for coming back," she whispered.

Her breathing slowed, then it stopped altogether.

Eddie touched her. She was cold.

"Shit, don't be dead now," he said.

The zombies were closing in. Eddie was reaching for the gear shift when Sue Ann sat up again, facing Eddie. Her lips peeled back into thin pale lines of flesh as she opened her mouth, expelling thick, foamy drool.

Eddie threw himself against the door, trying to get away. Sue Ann lunged at him, her jaws snapping, and somewhere from the back of her throat came the agonized wail of the living dead. . . .

TWELVE

Edna's cafe was packed with civilians and military. The noise level was unbearable. Edgewater sat at the counter with a cup of coffee. Edna and Abigail were running food orders without stopping to breathe.

Sheriff Colbrook came into the cafe and made a beeline for Edgewater. "We need to talk," he said, taking the stool beside Edgewater.

Edgewater gave him a sideways glance. "About what?"

"You serious?" Colbrook asked. "About the situation we're in and what you're going to do about it."

Edgewater sipped his coffee. "What can I do about it, son? The situation is out of control. You saw it with your own two goddamned eyes. Hell, take a look at the news. The black shit's got people dropping like flies and coming back quicker than you can drop your trousers and take a dump. We're up to our necks in dead things."

"That's all you have? All your bravado and that mightier-than-thou bullshit, and that's all you have to offer?"

Edgewater lit a cigar. "I got men posted all around the perimeter of this godforsaken town. We'll keep the dead sons of bitches out. That's about all I can do for you and your town. The rest of the goddamned country is on its own at this point."

Colbrook looked at Edgewater for a long moment, considering what else he could say. Edgewater didn't bother looking back at him. As far as Colbrook could see, the military's official capacity was coming to an end.

"Have a nice day, Colonel," Colbrook said, then left.

Dalton was getting out of his truck when Colbrook came out of Edna's. He pulled a pack of cigarettes from his shirt pocket.

"Got another one of those?" Colbrook asked.

Dalton shook one loose. Colbrook lit it with his own lighter "Just talked to Edgewater. He says the military is pretty much finished."

"You believe that?"

"No choice but to believe it. I saw what the stuff from those rocks does. It isn't pretty, and with more dead people coming back by the minute, we're all pretty much screwed."

"What's the plan then?"

"Edgewater's got men posted around town. That'll do for now, but we're going to need something more secure and permanent. Any ideas you have right about now would be welcome."

"I'll give it some thought, see what I can come up with," Dalton said.

"In the meantime, let's see what we can find out on the news," Colbrook told him. "I'm not about to get all my information from Edgewater."

Colbrook wasn't sure there was anything he could do the military couldn't, but he wasn't prone to sitting on his ass and letting shit happen. If there was even a slight chance he could do anything to keep the people of Faith safe, he'd take that chance and play it for all it was worth.

THIRTEEN

"This is great, Johnny. You're a real rocket scientist. We should have stayed in the car."

"And what, wait for someone to come along and save our asses? I make my own fuckin' way. It works out better."

They were walking along the shoulder of a deserted stretch of highway. Rain came down in intermittent bursts. Wanda was out of breath and doing her best to keep up.

"Where do you think everybody's gone?"

"Probably holed up inside their houses, ready to blow away anything that comes near the front door. That's where the smart money is."

"Slow down, will ya?"

"You need to pick up the pace."

"What's the hurry?"

"In case you haven't noticed, we're in the dark with who the fuck knows what's goin' on, and pardon my fuckin' grammar, I don't want my balls on a platter like Swedish meatballs."

"I'm wearing' heels. You try walkin' in the rain on the shoulder of the highway in heels sometime, you'll see."

"No, thanks," Johnny said.

"I thought you put more gas in the car."

"When did I have time to turn on the pump? What did you expect me to do, tell the rabid kid to wait while I filled up?"

She sighed. "I'm tired of fighting, Johnny. Can we just stop?"

"That's the best idea I've heard all day."

"Hey, listen . . ." He stopped and cocked an ear. "You hear that?"

There was a low sound in the distance that gradually became identifiable as the sound of a vehicle, then a pair of headlights topped the hill behind them. Johnny stepped into the road and began waving his arms as a 1960s VW bus approached. The mini-bus made no effort to slow as it reached them and roared past, almost clipping Johnny in the process. He spun around to flip the finger at the mini-bus and saw the taillights brighten as the VW slowed and pulled to the shoulder of the road.

Johnny took off at a sprint, grateful to see the mini-bus backing up to meet them, and Wanda did her best to keep up, twisting her ankle in the process. The mini-bus stopped and the side door slid open. Johnny helped Wanda in, then he climbed in behind her and pulled the door shut.

"Appreciate the ride," Johnny said. "Even if you did almost run me over."

"Sorry about that," the kid behind the wheel said.

He couldn't have been more than twenty, with a head full of curly blonde hair and a goofy grin. A blonde hippie chick, probably younger than the driver, sat in the passenger seat.

"Wow, you guys are, like, soaked," the kid said.

"That shit tends to happen when you're walkin' in the rain," Johnny said.

Wanda jabbed him with her elbow and gave him a dirty look, but it really didn't matter. His sarcasm had gone over the kid's head.

"We appreciate the lift," Wanda said, adding more sincerity to make up for Johnny's lack of manners.

"No problem," the hippie chick said. "We couldn't leave you stranded out there. Sorry we drove by at first, but with everything going on, like, we had to be careful, ya know."

"I don't blame you," Wanda said.

"My name's Terri Lynn, by the way, and this is my boyfriend Bobby."

"I'm Wanda and this is my *rude* friend Johnny, who sometimes doesn't know when to stop runnin' his mouth. Sorry about that."

"Don't apologize for me," Johnny said.

"It's cool, really," Terri Lynn said. "So, where are you two heading?"

"Not a fuckin' clue," Johnny said. "Somewhere where everything isn't fuckin' nuts, that's all I care about."

"That would be far out, man, but I don't think there's any place like that. The whole country's under the influence of bad, bad karma right now."

"Is that what you call it?" Johnny said, nearing the end of his rope. "You think this is all some kinda bad karma?"

Terri Lynn took a plastic bag full of weed and a package of rolling papers from the glove box and began rolling a joint.

"Dead people, man," Bobby said. "It's just like in the movies."

"This ain't the movies," Johnny told him. "You keep gettin' your panties wet like you are, you ain't gonna last long."

"We came down from Canada," Bobby went on, completely oblivious to Johnny's comment. "My dad owns a funeral home outside of Detroit. Bright Funeral Home. Bright's the family name. I could've owned it, but man . . ."

Johnny rolled his eyes and sighed.

"Terri and me went by to see if he was okay," Bobby went on. "I'm tellin' you, those dead things were everywhere, and my old man was one of 'em."

Terri passed the joint to Bobby. He took it from her and filled his lungs with the acrid smoke, almost choking in his effort to keep it in, then reached back to offer the joint to Johnny.

"I don't need that shit," Johnny said. "I see dead people without it."

Bobby offered it to Wanda, who shook her head. He shrugged and handed it to Terri.

"Get off at the next exit," Johnny said. "We need some guns."

"Man, we don't need guns," Bobby said.

"Have you lost your fuckin' mind, kid? If we plan on surviving, we're gonna need some guns."

"There are other ways to stay safe," Terri Lynn said. "That's what the police and the military are for."

"Smokin' that shit has really messed up your mind," Johnny told her. "Let me tell you somethin', sister, you depend on those

63

people if you want, but when the shit hits the fan, I'm the only one I'm countin' on to save my ass. Now, pull off the fuckin' highway and let's find some guns."

The next exit came less than half a mile later. Bobby pulled off the highway and made a right. He drove for a mile before they came to a small town. A few of the houses were lit. Most of them looked deserted, with windows busted out and trash strewn everywhere.

"Wow, does this place look dead or what?" Bobby said.

"Nice choice of words, flower child," Johnny said. He leaned between the seats to look out the front window. "Take a right at the end of the street."

Bobby slowed and came to a stop at the intersection, making sure to activate his blinker. He made a right and drove until the residential buildings began to thin out, giving way to a small-town business section.

"Over there," Johnny said, pointing at a building with a sign that read: MARTY'S ONE-STOP SPORTING SHOP.

Bobby slowed to a stop and put the mini-bus in park.

Johnny slid the side door open and hopped out. Bobby looked at Terri, shrugged his shoulders, and got out to join Johnny. Johnny was a little worried about how pale and weak the kid looked, but he was Johnny's backup, like it or not.

"Lock the doors and honk if you get into trouble," Johnny told Wanda.

"Hey, Johnny," she said.

"Yeah?" he said.

"Be careful."

Johnny smiled a genuine smile. "I always am," he said, then shut the door and waited until he heard it lock before he turned away.

The store was locked up tight, so Johnny picked up a nearby rock and hurled it through the plate glass window. He kicked shards of glass out of the way and climbed through the window, waving for Bobby to follow him. Once inside, he said, "Look for guns, knives, ammunition, anything you think we can use."

A glass case on one side of the store housed a wide selection of handguns. Johnny smashed the case, grabbed three guns, then went around behind the counter. He found a bag and tossed the guns inside, then he went through the ammunition and found everything he could use.

"How 'bout these?" Bobby asked, grinning big as he held up an armload of first aid kits.

"That's what I'm talkin' about, kid," Johnny said. He pushed the weapons and ammo across the counter. "Take this stuff to the van. I'm grabbin' some rifles. I'll be right behind you."

When Bobby was outside, Johnny went through the store, gathering up flashlights, batteries, a hunting rifle, and a couple of shotguns. He was in the process of loading another bag with ammunition when the horn on the mini-bus began to go crazy.

Johnny hurried to look outside. A swarm of dead things were crawling all over the mini-bus. Johnny dropped everything to the floor except a shotgun, then he dropped to his knees and went through the stuff until he found a box of shells for the shotgun. He loaded quickly, emptied the remaining shells from the box into his pocket, and stepped outside.

A dead waitress was banging her head on the passenger side of the mini-bus. "Hey, sweet cheeks," Johnny said.

She turned toward the sound of his voice. He leveled the shotgun, bringing its business end within inches of the dead girl's face, and squeezed off a round. Her head exploded in a shower of blood and bone fragment.

Johnny swung left, dropping the shotgun down to waist level. An old man in coveralls was limping toward him. Johnny fired and nearly blew the man in half, but he kept coming anyway, dragging his internal organs with him. Johnny didn't miss a beat as he raised the shotgun and fired again, disintegrating the old man's head.

"Open the fuckin' door," Johnny yelled.

The side door slid open and Wanda leaned out, trying to lend Johnny a hand. "Come on, Johnny," He started to climb in, remembered the supplies at the front door, and turned around for them. Two dead things came around the front of the VW.

65

Johnny half-turned toward them and fired twice. He missed the first shot entirely. The second shot blew the head off one of the dead things. By then, the other one was almost on him, leaving Johnny no choice but to abandon the supplies. He jumped into the mini-bus, slammed the door shut, and said, "Go, damnit, and run over anything that gets in your way."

Bobby hit the gas. A naked man with his ribcage exposed ran in front of the VW, causing Bobby to freeze up.

"Hit the fuckin' thing," Johnny said.

Bobby closed his eyes and pressed his foot down on the pedal. There was a solid thump as the VW hit the zombie, knocking it to the ground, and a slight jolt as the VW rolled over it.

Bobby made a U-turn, took out a mailbox, and drove onto the sidewalk.

Johnny reloaded the shotgun, trying to keep his balance as Bobby whipped the mini-bus all over the place.

"Gimme the fuckin' wheel," Johnny said.

Bobby slammed on the brakes and switched places with Johnny.

"This is how you do it," Johnny said, laying the shotgun on the floor.

He hit the gas, squealing tires against the pavement as he set the front of the VW in line with the biggest cluster of walking stiffs he could find. The little VW took a beating as it plowed through the corpses, throwing rotting body parts in every direction.

"Motherfuckers," Johnny said, grinning as he checked his handiwork in the rearview mirror. "Let's see how easy it is to walk now."

FOURTEEN

The sun was already shining bright. It was going to be another hot one, but a cool early-morning breeze kept the heat under control for now.

Edna's place was teeming with activity. Joe was in the kitchen, filling orders as fast as he could. Edna and Abigail did the best they could to keep up with the customers.

One of the soldiers—a young private—patted Abigail on the ass when she walked by. Two of his buddies laughed and snorted like pigs.

"Do that again and I swear I'll knock you out of that booth," Abigail said.

The laughing soldiers stopped laughing and stared at Abby with their mouths still hanging open. The private who'd smacked her ass suddenly looked ashamed of himself. His face turned red.

"Sorry about that, ma'am. I really am," he said. "I didn't mean nothing by it, really. Just letting off a little steam is all."

Abigail stared at him hard for another moment, then said, "Don't let it happen again," and walked away.

* * *

Colbrook, Dalton, Edgewater, and deputies Hagerman and Swanson were at the Sheriff's Office. They'd been discussing the situation in heated fashion for some time. To everybody's surprise, Edgewater was along for the ride, though his big dick status seemed to be alive and well.

"All right, let's hear this bright idea you yokels have concocted," he said, filling the air with a cloud of cigar smoke.

The Sheriff nodded at Dalton, inviting him to take the floor. Dalton, who had been leaning against a desk with his arms crossed, straightened up and cleared his throat. "We want to build a wall around Faith," he said.

67

Edgewater stared at him for a long time, then said, "That's it? You want to build a fucking wall? That's your big plan?"

"That's it," Dalton said.

Edgewater's face remained impassive for what seemed an eternity, then a grin slowly spread across his face. He chuckled, then broke into a hearty laugh. "Well, fuck me runnin', I like it. We can do that shit." He clapped Dalton on the shoulder. "Son of a bitch, you boys might be military material after all."

* * *

Edgewater instructed his men to work with the people of Faith. He let them know he expected one hundred percent, and if he didn't get it, there would be hell to pay and he'd be collecting the bill.

On the second day of construction, just before the finishing touches were in place, Pvt. Hawkins, the soldier who'd patted Abigail's ass, was leaning against a post, smoking a cigarette and drinking a can of soda.

"Get your ass in gear, private," Edgewater barked. "Show some fuckin' ambition or I'll put my boot so far up your ass you'll shine it with your prostate."

A siren went off, saving Hawkins from an embarrassing situation.

"Rotten meat heading our way," Edgewater yelled.

Two tanks rolled to the edge of the perimeter, surrounded by several foot soldiers armed and ready for the fight.

After seeing to the placement of troops, Edgewater said to Colbrook, "You and your boys sweep the town and blow anybody away that ain't breathin' the right way."

Colbrook nodded and was about to gather his deputies when he saw a horde of at least a hundred walking corpses making their way down a mountain ridge south of town. The tanks and troops were focused on a much smaller group of corpses.

"Over there," Colbrook said to Edgewater.

"Fuckers are on the warpath," Edgewater said, his eyes gleaming with excitement as he followed Colbrook's direction.

He keyed his radio. "Turn those tanks south and blast the side of that mountain."

The tanks repositioned on Edgewater's command. The first 120 mm round left one tank's smooth bore cannon and whistled through the air, on a collision course with the side of the mountain. The second tank joined the attack and the rounds slammed into the mountainside, disintegrating large quantities of dead flesh.

"Holy Christ, that's the glory of love. Nail 'em again," Edgewater ordered.

Colbrook said to his deputies, "You two ride together. Cover as much ground as you can. Shoot anybody that looks like they might be infected."

"What if we can't tell?" Hagerman asked.

"Then you shoot 'em to be on the safe side," Edgewater chimed in.

Hagerman and Swanson looked to the Sheriff for confirmation.

"Do what he says," Colbrook said, then to Dalton, "You coming with me?"

"I'm in," Dalton said.

As the four of them headed out, Edgewater and his troops continued fighting off advancing zombies, which were now coming from the North as well as the south. The soldiers fanned out, meeting the zombies with a hail of M-16 fire. Most of the gun fire did nothing more than hold the walking dead at bay, but the occasional headshot brought some of them down.

* * *

"Slow down," Terri Lynn said. "There's something going on up there."

"I see it," Johnny replied sharply, showing his irritation.

They'd passed several signs pointing to a town called Faith. At Johnny's best guess, they should almost be there. He slowed down to exit the highway and a military jeep met them at the bottom of the exit.

Columns of black smoke rose in the distance, beyond a large wooden structure that appeared to be blocking off an entire town.

The military vehicle pulled alongside the VW. One of the soldiers motioned for Johnny to roll down the window.

"What's goin' on, guys?" Johnny asked, trying to keep it friendly.

"We're at war," the soldier in the passenger seat said. "Don't it look like a war to you?"

That was all Johnny could take. He was fed up with idiots. "Look, wiseass," he said. "I got two women and another guy in here. We just wanna get somewhere we can settle in. We got weapons, so if you need a hand, we can pitch in."

The driver said, "Get the colonel on the horn, see what he says."

The passenger-seat soldier didn't look too happy, but he keyed the mic. "Come in, Colonel Edgewater," he said.

"Go," Edgewater came back immediately.

"We have four civilians detained at the east edge of town. Two men, two women. Please advise."

The radio gave a burst of static, followed by Edgewater's voice. "Are they alive and able bodied?"

"Yes, sir, alive and able bodied. They say they have weapons and are willing to fight."

"Then you send their asses right through," Edgewater said.

"Roger that, Colonel," the soldier said. He hung the mic up. "Your lucky day," he said to Johnny. "You just joined the United States Army."

Johnny followed the jeep to the entrance of Faith. A front gate swung open and both vehicles passed through. Once inside, the jeep made a U-turn and headed out again.

Johnny lit a cigarette and took time to look around. Faith appeared to be the New Mecca. There were military vehicles everywhere—tanks and helicopters and trucks, all carrying weapons and soldiers.

"This is where we wanna be," Johnny said.

He wasn't sure where he was going, so he followed Main Street and made a right at the first stoplight. Wanda, Terri Lynn, and Bobby pressed their faces to the windows to get a better look at all the activity. Something whistled overhead, followed by a godawful explosion.

"Jesus, Johnny, you brought us into the middle of World War Three," Wanda said.

"In case you hadn't noticed, the world's gone south, baby. World War Three would be a cakewalk compared to the neck-deep shit we're in."

"This is a bad trip," Terri Lynn said. "A real bad trip."

"Get used to it," Johnny said.

He drove until the military congestion made it impossible to go any further, then he parked the VW and got out. Wanda was next, followed by Bobby. Terri Lynn decided she was staying in the mini-bus.

Johnny took one look at Edgewater across the street and knew that was the man to see. He could spot a man in charge a hundred miles away, and that motherfucker was boss man.

Edgewater caught sight of Johnny at about the same time as Johnny saw him. The two of them met in the middle of the street, each strutting like a rooster claiming a hen house.

"You the new recruits?" Edgewater said.

"Wat's that?" Johnny asked.

"You just get here? That's what I'm askin', son."

"Yeah, we just met the welcoming committee," Johnny replied.

"Can't be too goddamned careful," Edgewater said. "We like to keep it tight. Don't get too comfortable, you hear me? We're in the middle of a fucking war and there's no time to shit, shower, or shave." He paused long enough to give Johnny the once over. "You look like a troublemaker to me. Are you a troublemaker?"

"If I get pushed," Johnny said.

"Well, son, the military is in charge here. You don't like the rules, you can get right down the fucking road. You got that?"

"I ain't in the military," Johnny said. "I work for myself."

"I ain't askin' you to work for me, son, just saying we won't tolerate any bullshit. You wanna make trouble, you go handle the fucking dead things on your own time."

A burst of static from Edgewater's radio interrupted his initiation speech, followed by a panicked soldier.

"Colonel, sir, they're picking up weapons," the soldier said.

"Come again," Edgewater responded.

"The corpses are shooting us with our own arms, sir," the soldier replied.

Edgewater keyed his radio. "How the hell are they getting our weapons? Do not, I repeat, *do not* let them get their grubby hands on our goddamned weapons, is that clear?"

"Colonel, sir, we're doing our . . . aaagghhhh . . ."

Edgewater shook his head in disgust, slipped his radio back in its pouch, and turned his attention back to Johnny. "You see what I'm up against here?" He glanced over Johnny's shoulder at the VW, where Wanda, Bobby, and now even Terri Lynn were waiting for direction. "That your rag-tag bunch eyeballin' us?"

"Yeah, those are my friends," Johnny said.

"I want their asses armed and dangerous. Everybody in this fuckin' camp will be ready to fight. You ain't in Kansas anymore, son."

"I ain't from Kansas," Johnny said, then turned on his heels and strode away from the colonel before he could mouth off again.

* * *

"The Steinbergers live here," Colbrook said.

He and Dalton were standing in front of a cozy little yellow house with a colorful flower bed in the front yard. The front door was wide open.

"Real old couple," Colbrook said. "Pretty much keep to themselves." He cleared his throat. "Martha, Franklin, you okay in there?"

He glanced at Dalton, shaking his head slowly, indicating he didn't have a good feeling about what they were going to find.

"We better just go in," Dalton said.

"Yeah, I guess we better," Colbrook agreed. "I mean, these folks *never* leave their house. They even have their groceries delivered."

The sheriff started toward the entrance of the house, with Dalton close behind. The sheriff's hand hovered over the butt of his Smith and Wesson.

Something moved in the back of the house as soon as they entered. Colbrook unsnapped his holster and drew his gun. He gave Dalton a nervous glance and made his way toward the noise.

"Anybody here?" he called, not expecting an answer.

The first room they came to was a small bedroom dominated by a large antique bed. The door was slightly ajar. Deep shadows made it impossible to see into the room. Colbrook placed a hand against the door and readied himself to enter.

"Now I wish I'd brought the shotgun," Dalton whispered.

Colbrook nodded agreement, took a deep breath, and pushed the door open. Franklin was sitting on the floor just inside the room. His wife's half-devoured head was in his lap. Strings of bloody flesh hung from his lips; his face was flecked with bits of what could only be some of what Martha used to think with.

"Holy Jesus," Colbrook said.

"Over there," Dalton said, nodding to where a pale, wrinkled arm protruded from beneath the bed.

Colbrook glanced at the arm and turned his attention back to Franklin, not wanting to let his guard down.

"You know what I have to do, right, Dalton?"

"I know what you have to do," Dalton said.

Before Colbrook could bring himself to shoot, Franklin lunged at him. Martha's head fell to the floor and rolled off somewhere. Colbrook didn't see where it went because he was too busy backing out of the room, bumping into Dalton in the process.

"Out, go," he shouted, pushing Dalton as he continued backpedalling.

They made it out of the room. Colbrook slammed the door. Franklin collided with it on the other side.

"We're going to have to open it again," Colbrook said. "I've got to put him down."

"Guess so," Dalton agreed, but without any real enthusiasm.

"Count of three," Colbrook said.

"Wait," Dalton said.

"For what?"

"Just stallin', I guess."

"Dalton, damnit . . ."

"Okay, let's do it."

He counted fast and kicked the door. It hit Franklin, knocking him back into the room. Colbrook rushed into the room, raising his gun as Franklin came at him faster than he'd ever moved in life.

"Sorry, old man," Colbrook said.

He squeezed off a round that drilled into Franklin's forehead. Franklin halted in mid step, jerked twice, and dropped to the ground.

Colbrook stood for several seconds without moving, his gun still aimed where Franklin had been standing only moments earlier.

Dalton looked into the closet. "I found the rest of Martha," he said.

* * *

The last gunshots and explosions rang out as a major battle of the war for Faith came to an end. Corpses adorned the landscape north and south of Faith. Some were twice dead, others were visiting for the first time. Zombies and soldiers alike, now hard to distinguish between the two. Those lucky enough to be blown to pieces stayed down. Some of them walked again, ready for the next round.

Edgewater was on the radio. "Pull back," he ordered. "We've lost too many in this skirmish. Let's cut our losses here and, by God, regroup."

He cussed himself in hushed tones as troops began to roll back into town. It pissed him off to have to pull back. The idea of giving up ground to those disgusting, rotting corpses was like a corn cob up his ass. It simply wasn't the American way, but it was the best battle strategy he had at the moment. The more goddamned soldiers that dropped with their heads still intact, the more fucking dead things there were to contend with, and that just wouldn't do.

Edgewater saw some of his able bodied soldiers tending to the wounded. Christ in a hand basket, what the fuck was that all about?

He strode across the street with fire in his eyes, nearly trembling with anger. "Shoot any-goddamn-body that's been bitten, scratched, or even looked at hard by one of those things," he barked as he reached the group. "I don't give a damn if your bleeding heart thinks they can make it or not, we can't afford to have 'em gettin' up and walkin' around."

His men looked up at him with confusion written on their faces. Some still held their bleeding comrades in their arms.

"But, Colonel—" Private Daybrook began.

"Don't but me, Private. I said kill every one of 'em."

To make his point, Edgewater drew his .45 and leveled it at one of the wounded soldiers. "That a shoulder wound you got there, son?" he said, overly dramatized for everybody within earshot. "Let me help you."

He squeezed the trigger, blowing the soldier's brains across the pavement, then he turned to Private Daybrook. "I suggest you grab your family jewels in one hand and your gun in another. Kill or be killed, Private, are we fuckin' clear?"

"We're clear, Sir," Private Daybrook said.

"Damn good," Edgewater replied, holstering his .45 as he strode away to the musical sound of gunfire.

FIFTEEN

Colbrook looked like death warmed over. His eyes were red and rimmed with dark circles, and he was as pale as any one of those dead things.

Sarah came up behind him and placed a hand on his shoulder. "You doing okay?" she asked.

"A little tired is all."

"You look more than a little tired," she said.

She began rubbing his temples. He closed his eyes and enjoyed the way it felt. When he opened his eyes again, Sarah was watching him. Something passed between them that neither could deny. It was a hell of a time for such feelings, but they were there nonetheless.

Colbrook sat up, then stood and took Sarah into his arms. He let a proper moment pass before he kissed her.

"I've been waiting for that a long time," she said when the kiss ended.

"Have you?"

"Oh yes, Sheriff Colbrook, a long time."

They kissed again, this time with more intensity. His hands slid over the front of her uniform and fumbled with the buttons.

"Let's lock the door," he said.

After locking the door, Colbrook cleared a desk with one sweep of his arm, sending everything onto the floor. He lifted Sarah and went to work on her clothes, disrobing her in record time.

She fell back on the desk, pulling him down with her, panting and gasping between kisses. She got his belt undone and his pants and briefs below his ass, then he was between her legs, groaning as her soft fingers stroked his cock and guided him into her.

76

The sex was hot, fast, and verging on violent. Maybe it was the desperation of the moment, maybe it was a sudden new outlook on taking advantage of life while there was still life to take advantage of. Whatever the reason, they devoured one another. When it was over, they lay together on the desk, neither of them breathing steady for several minutes.

"Is it ever going to be the same again?" Sarah finally asked.

"I don't know about that," Colbrook said. He kissed her on the forehead. "I wish I had an answer for you."

"I feel so cheated," Sarah said. "All this time I've wanted you, and when I finally get what I want, it's in the middle of a living nightmare."

"I know what you mean," Colbrook said. "This whole thing—zombies, Edgewater, the military rolling through town like it's some war-torn country, I don't know how much more of it I can take."

They were silent for a long while. Every so often there was the sporadic sound of gunfire outside.

"I killed people today, Sarah," Colbrook said. "Not live people, no. They were dead, but they were neighbors. People I've shopped with, nodded to on the street, hell, some I've even fished with and played cards with. I had to look into their eyes and blow their heads off."

"You did what you had to do, Jeff."

"I know that. The worst part is, I'm okay with it. I'm okay with it because when I looked into their eyes, all I saw was nothing."

Sarah didn't know how to respond to that, so she didn't. She pulled Jeff Colbrook close and held him tight, letting him bury his face against her breasts. There was more sporadic gunfire, then silence except for the sound of Jeff Colbrook shedding tears for a life that may never again be right.

SIXTEEN

Edgewater sat at the counter in Edna's, digging into a big plate of food and oblivious to everyone around him. That's the way it would seem to anyone looking, but Edgewater was never oblivious. He knew everything going on around him. It was his business to be aware.

The cafe was crowded, mostly with tired soldiers lucky enough to grab a meal away from the battle zone. Dalton and Jed occupied a corner table.

Johnny, Wanda, Bobby, and Terri Lynn were in a booth nearby. Although they'd been accepted into the town, they still felt like outsiders.

"Here you go," Abigail said, setting food in front of Jed and Dalton.

"Thanks, Abby," Dalton said.

"You're welcome."

Their eyes met briefly and Abigail blushed.

"Order up," Edna Jean shouted.

"I better go," Abigail said. She started to turn away, hesitated, then said, "Can I see you later?"

"Sure thing," Dalton said. "Meet you after you're through here?"

"Can you give me a lift home?"

"You bet."

He watched Abigail head back to the kitchen. Jed caught the look on Dalton's face. It had been a long time since Jed had experienced such a feeling as what Dalton was experiencing, but he recognized it all the same.

"There's love in the air, I'll tell ya that," Jed noted. "Young'un's got a thing for you, if you ain't too blind to see it, Dalton."

"I see it fine," Dalton said. "Being cautious is all."

"Well, throw it to the wind. We might all be livin' on a short string, if you get my meaning. Make the most of the time you got. That's my advice, if you're interested."

"It's good advice," Dalton said. "I just might take it to heart."

"You do that. Sometimes an old coot knows best."

Dalton watched as Abigail was gathering orders. She brushed a strand of blonde hair behind one ear. That single move was enough to make Dalton's heart do all those funny things a heart does when everything's good.

"Sometimes an old coot does know best," Dalton said. "I believe that."

SEVENTEEN

While new love blossomed in the town of Faith and the dead were momentarily repelled, those in surrounding communities were not so lucky. The survivors (and there were few) in those surrounding communities sought shelter wherever they could, waiting it out as their dead spewed forth into the world, many on a collision course with Faith.

Billy Evans was one of those survivors. He was fifteen years old and holed up in a root cellar beneath the country farmhouse he'd shared with his mother, father, and sister. They were all dead now, and though Billy didn't know it, shambling along the road to Faith at this very moment.

Billy had managed to grab his daddy's Mossberg shotgun and a box of rounds. He knew how to use the shotgun, which he was grateful for. His daddy had seen to it.

It was dark in the cellar. Billy wasn't sure how long he'd been cooped up there. Except for the occasional foray into the house for something to eat or drink, he hadn't been out in several days. He'd found an old bucket to relieve himself in when the need arose, which made for an awful stench that Billy wished he didn't have to smell.

He couldn't stay in the cellar forever. He knew that much for sure. Where he'd go when he left was still a mystery. Before his family had been attacked and devoured by a horde of dead things, they had all planned to head up north. He wasn't sure why his daddy had decided on north, but that had been the plan.

Billy couldn't think beyond getting out of Little Creek, which was about as far as he'd ever been, not counting the time his daddy had taken him to Faith to an American Indian festival.

Faith seemed like forever away to him. It was actually only fifteen miles, but to Billy, that might as well be halfway across the world.

He had to try, though. He was running out of food, he was going crazy in the dark, and he couldn't stand the smell of the bucket.

He finally made his decision. He wasn't going to stay in the cellar any longer. What was waiting for him out there in the world wasn't very good, but it seemed like a better option to him than waiting in the cellar for what was wandering around in the world to find him.

He grabbed the shotgun, which he did every time he left the cellar, and he opened the cellar door. It was daylight. He was thankful for that much. Not that he wasn't going to be wandering around at night, but at least he could start his journey in the daylight.

He made one last stop inside the house to see what he could scrounge up to take with him. He found some stale crackers and warm soda. He stuffed them into a backpack, slung the pack over his shoulder, and started in the direction he was sure Faith was in. He didn't know what would be waiting for him there, but he hoped he'd find people who were still alive. That was the thing he wanted more than anything in the world.

It was three miles to the nearest main road. Billy walked a good portion of it without incident. He spent most of that time thinking about his daddy and his momma and his sister. His sister, mostly, because she had been the first to go, with Billy just a few feet away from her. He'd tried to save her, but there were so many of those things. The whole town, it seemed like, had decided to have dinner at his house.

When he was almost to the main road (that's the only name he knew to call it), he began seeing some of the dead things moving around. They were pretty far away at first, but when they began to notice him one by one, they started making their way in his direction.

He picked up the pace to keep ahead of them, but had the shotgun clutched tight in his hands just in case.

When he was almost to the top of the slope leading to the main road, he looked back over his shoulder to make sure the things were staying behind him. He was so busy looking back that he didn't see the massive dead thing rising in front of him, and when he ran into it, he felt like he'd hit a brick wall. He went tumbling back down the slope, head over heels, still gripping the shotgun in both hands, praying it didn't go off.

He reached the bottom of the hill and knew at once that his ankle was twisted. The zombie was coming down the slope. He thought he recognized the dead man as a deaf-mute drifter that worked on some of the local farms whenever there was extra work to be had. The guy really didn't look all that dead, unless you counted the hole in the side of his neck and the fact that one of his arms had been chewed off at the elbow, leaving nothing behind but strands of bloody tissue that swung back and forth as he made his way down the slope.

Billy drew himself into a sitting position. He knew the Mossberg was going to knock him back, so he had to make the first shot count. He raised the barrel of the shotgun with his left hand and tightened his finger on the trigger, making sure to account for the fact that he was lower than his target. One shot, that was it. One shot, and if he missed, Mr. Deaf-mute was going to have a field day with him.

He sighted in on the zombie's head, thankful it was a big target, then he squeezed the trigger. Just like he knew, the kick from the shotgun rammed his shoulder and sent him flying backward. After a few seconds to recover, he sat up to see how he'd done.

There was no sign of Mr. Deaf-mute at first, then he saw the lump on the ground, partially hidden by a mass of overgrown weeds. He couldn't see if he'd taken the head off or not, but since the dead thing seemed to be staying dead, he thought maybe he'd done a pretty good job.

The immediate problem was out of the way. There was another problem looming behind him. The walking corpses he'd managed to keep ahead of were now closing in on him.

With his bad ankle, there was no way he was going to get ahead of them again.

He started back up the slope, crawling at first, and when he realized that wasn't going to get him anywhere fast, he forced himself to stand on his hurt ankle. The pain was fierce, sending jolts of what felt like electricity up his leg. He managed to stay on his feet despite the pain and started up the hill, not quite moving at the pace he wanted, but doing much better than when he was crawling.

He realized his ankle had to be almost broken. He'd never had a twisted ankle that delivered this much pain. He tried not to look down at it because he didn't want to know the truth, but he looked anyway, and saw that his foot was twisted almost 360 degrees.

He reached the top of the slope and collapsed, but he kept going, holding the shotgun in one hand as he dragged himself to the center of the road. He rolled over when he could go no further. Several of the zombies had topped the slope and were moving toward him.

He thought he heard something in the distance. He tried to get the shotgun into position, but there were five or six corpses coming his way. There wasn't any chance he could get more than one of them before they were on top of him.

The distant sound grew louder. Billy recognized it as a car, maybe even a truck, and it sounded like the engine was revving up. Sure enough, it was a car. A station wagon, to be exact, and it was barreling this way, on a direct collision course with the dead things coming at him.

He saw the front of the station wagon slam into the zombies and heard the squeal of tires as the car came to a halt. The driver's side door flew open and a tall, wide man with disheveled blonde hair got out, opening fire with what appeared to be a machine gun. Some of the zombies that hadn't been taken out with the car took several bursts from the machine gun as the blonde man helped Billy to his feet.

"In the car," the blond man said.

"My ankle," Billy said.

The man took one look at Billy's ankle, turned and released a burst of gunfire on two more walking corpses, then squatted and wrapped a thick arm around Billy's legs.

Jim Pierce (formerly Pastor Jim Pierce) was in his fifties, but he still had the strength of an ox. He hefted Billy (who still clutched his shotgun) over his shoulder and carried him to the car, pushing him across the seat as he climbed in behind the wheel.

"Hold on," Jim Pierce said, but he didn't give Billy time to heed the warning. He didn't even bother closing the car door. He mashed his foot down on the gas pedal and plowed through a couple of corpses that looked like they'd been buried for the better part of the century.

"Thank you, mister," Billy said.

"Jim. Call me Jim."

"I'm Billy."

"How'd you end up in a tight spot like that, Billy?"

"Tryin' to get somewhere safe. I was doin' all right 'til I hurt my ankle."

"Where are your parents?"

"Dead. My sister too."

"I'm sorry to hear that."

"It's okay," Billy said, then after a pause, "How'd this happen?"

"I don't really know," Jim said.

He glanced over at the boy, wishing he could give an answer, but there was nothing to say. Nothing that would bring the kid's parents back or make their deaths more meaningful. Nothing that would make the things either of them had seen make sense.

"Where we gonna go, Jim?" Billy asked.

Jim shrugged. "The first place that looks like we might stand a chance, I guess. Where that might be, your guess is good as mine."

They rode in silence for several minutes, then Billy said, "Where'd you come from? Where were you when this happened, I mean?"

"I was getting ready to talk about God," Jim Pierce said. "Same as I always do. I was the pastor of a church in Canton. My congregation . . ."

Billy was a smart kid. When Jim Pierce let the words trail off, Billy knew exactly what that meant.

"I never knew a preacher could use a gun like you do," Billy said.

The former Pastor Jim Pierce chuckled. "Neither did I, Billy. I found it in the back room of the local gun shop and gave myself a crash course. Figured I'd leave the rest up to God. Seemed liked as good a plan as any."

Jim Pierce fell into silence, contemplating the events of the last few days. It still weighed heavy on him that he'd left Canton. Not very Godly, leaving behind the neighbors he'd preached to every Wednesday and Sunday, but he'd done all he could do. Those who could get away did. The others died. Some of those who died came back.

"You okay?" Billy asked.

Jim looked at him again, smiled, and said, "About as okay as I can be under the circumstances, I guess."

When they came to the outskirts of Faith, Billy looked in wonder at the corpses scattered around the landscape, while Jim admired the wall surrounding the town.

"Wow, something big happened here," Billy said.

"Looks like we found ground zero," Jim said.

"What's ground zero?"

Jim was about to answer, but his attention was drawn to a military transport truck moving in their direction. He angled his station wagon toward the truck and slowed until coming to a stop alongside the truck.

"How many in there?" the soldier behind the wheel of the truck asked.

"Just me and a boy," Jim said.

"You armed?"

"We have guns," Jim said.

The soldier keyed his radio. "Colonel, we have two survivors."

"Bring 'em in," Edgewater's voice boomed over the radio.

EIGHTEEN

D alton pulled into Abigail's driveway, leaving the truck running and the headlights on.

"We're here," he said, and immediately felt stupid for stating the obvious.

"Yep, we're here," she said, then after a short pause, "Can you stay?"

"I can do that," he said, happy for the invitation.

He followed Abigail inside, running possible scenarios through his mind as he did. He really liked this girl, but he didn't have a clue how to act around her, which only made him feel clumsy.

"Make yourself comfortable," she said, motioning to the couch.

Dalton sat.

"I'll be just a minute," she said, disappearing down a narrow hallway Dalton guessed led to her bedroom.

While Dalton waited for her to come back, he looked around the living room, taking in the little unicorn knick-knacks and the snow globes on shelves all over the room. It occurred to him that he'd known Abby for several years and had no idea she liked unicorns and snow globes. That made him even more nervous, and suddenly he wondered what he was doing here, sitting in her living room like a love-struck schoolboy.

Abby returned shortly, wearing a T-shirt and cut-off blue jean shorts. A sight for sore eyes on any day, but at this particular time, with everything going on like it was, Dalton couldn't think of anything he'd rather look at than Abigail in those shorts.

She sat beside him on the couch and turned to face Dalton, tucking her feet under her bottom. "I'm not what you'd call a bold girl, Dalton Connors," she said, wasting no time. "Not when it comes to matters of the heart, or anything else, for that matter."

Dalton listened. He felt like he should take some of the weight of the moment off her shoulders and take over, but he let her go on.

"I've waited to say this for a long time now, so hear me out."

"I will," he told her.

"I've dropped hints, but I guess they weren't good enough, or maybe you're just too blind to see them. I've done everything but throw myself at you, and now I guess I'm going to have to do that, because I feel like time is short. Do you know what I mean?"

Dalton knew exactly what she meant, and instead of letting her continue or putting her in the position of having to throw herself at him, he leaned over and kissed her lightly on the lips.

"I have feelings for you, Dalton. Strong feelings, and I know you probably think it's just infatuation or whatever, me being so much younger than you, but it's not. My feelings are—"

He cut her off. "Abby, I know I've been a little slow. I can see that. The way things are now, with the world falling apart around us, I don't want to waste any more time. None of us knows what tomorrow might bring. You're right about time being short. Life is short, Abby, and I don't want to waste another minute of it without finding out about us."

He leaned forward and kissed her again. It was a gentle brushing of lips at first, then more aggressive. They melted together, kissing like it was the first last kiss they would have together. When the kiss ended, Dalton brushed hair from Abigail's cheek and let his hand rest there.

"Will everything be all right?" she asked.

"We'll be all right," he said. "I don't know about everything else, but we'll be all right."

He took her in his arms and brought her close. They kissed again. His hands explored her body and his fingers fumbled with her clothing. They undressed one another awkwardly.

Dalton picked Abby up and carried her down the hallway, into the bedroom.

Their first round of lovemaking was urgent, with hands groping and their mouths locked in an almost-constant kiss. Abby guided Dalton into her, arching her back to take him as deep inside her as she could, as if making him a part of her would change everything.

Afterward, they lay together in silence, Dalton stroking Abby's hair from her face and letting the tips of his fingers trace her lips and eyes. They talked about the military presence and the rising dead. They talked about what might have been between them had they found one another before everything had gone to hell. Most of all, they talked about what it might be like if all of the insanity were to go away.

They made love again, with less intensity, reaching a place together where nothing existed but the two of them.

NINETEEN

The people of Faith, both those who had been born and raised there as well as those who found their way there, banded together. They saw changes no one could have imagined. A town normally content to take its place among other small towns of America was now a war zone.

"Our ship is sinking fast," Edgewater told Dalton, Colbrook, Johnny, and Jim one night over cold beers. "All my life, the military is all I ever gave a damn about. I'm a career military man. Never been any doubt about it. Now, the military is what we have here in this town. My command is all we can count on. The United States of America and its armed forces as we know it has gone to Hell. I've called in all the favors I can. We're on our own from here on out. You yokels are all I got left, save for the rest of my troops, and damnit, I guess that'll have to do."

"Appreciate your vote of confidence," Colbrook said.

"We've done all right so far," Dalton added. "We just need to keep working together, that's all."

"Working for what?" Johnny asked.

"For survival, you dimwit," Edgewater shot back.

"Look, I don't have to take your—"

"Stop it," Colbrook said. "The last thing we need to be doing is fighting with each other. In case you haven't noticed, the small portion of town we have left here is surrounded by corpses trying to suck us dry."

"He's right about that," Dalton agreed. "We start fighting amongst ourselves, we might as well go out there and join them."

Edgewater finished his beer and twisted the cap off another. To Johnny he said, "We may not see eye to eye, but I respect a man that's willing to stand up and fight. From what I've seen, you got a set of cojones on you big enough to bowl with. That makes you okay by me."

"I appreciate that," Johnny said. "I respect what you're doing here, and since we have the same goal in mind, it's probably best we work together."

"That's good," Edgewater said. "And now that we're finished wipin' each other's ass, let's get drunk."

The five men raised their beer bottles and drank.

"You know the world is going to hell when you're getting drunk with a man of God," Edgewater said, clapping a big hand on Jim Pierce's back.

"The way things are, I don't think God would deny me the right to a drink," Jim said.

"Never put a lot of faith in God myself," Edgewater said. "The way I see it, man is God. We need to take care of ourselves and stop relying on some unseen deity to do our dirty work." Edgewater paused long enough to take a drink of beer, then indicated the Uzi strapped across Jim's back. "You brought that weapon with you. Not standard issue for a man of God, I'd say, and I haven't seen you without it since you got here. Looks like you put your faith in more than God."

"I didn't say I relied on God for everything," Jim said.

"That's good, that's all I'm saying," Edgewater said. "You keep a little faith in God, that's no big deal, so long as you know when it comes down to it, God won't be holding your hand when you pull the trigger."

"Why is it you're always an asshole?" Colbrook asked Edgewater.

"It's in my nature, son," Edgewater said. "Born 'n' bred. A man never got far being nice. You're nice, people think they can take advantage of you. I've never had that problem."

"Gotta agree with the colonel on that one," Johnny said.

"Man knows the value of being an asshole," Edgewater replied, raising his beer bottle for a toast. "That's the kind of thinking that'll get us through this shit."

TWENTY

"Can I have some more pie?" Billy asked.

"Give the boy another piece of blueberry pie," Jed told Abigail. "You put it right on my tab."

"I'll bring him another piece of pie," Abby said. "And don't worry about any tab. The boy eats on the house, whatever he wants, Edna's orders."

"Well, nobody goes against Edna's orders, I know that much," Jed said.

"How about you? More coffee?"

Jed nodded. "And I'll take a piece of the blueberry myself."

Abby poured Jed's coffee, then went off to get the pie.

"Like I was tellin' ya," Jed said to Billy, "Dalton writes them cowboy books. Does a real fine job of it too. I always get me a signed copy."

While Jed went on about Dalton and his books, other patrons in Edna's place ate their meals and tried to pretend life was normal. It was less chaotic than before, with everybody in town, including the military, trying to work together.

In the kitchen, Edna and Joe discussed the short supply of food.

"How long have we got?" Edna asked.

"Maybe a day or two," Joe said. "We're running out of everything. Not just us, but everybody in town. Without supplies getting through, it won't be long before we're all starving."

"We'll have to shut down after today, Joe," Edna said. "I hate to do it, but we need to keep some set aside for rations."

"Generators are holding up for now, but they'll be gone too, once we run out of propane," Joe added.

"Colonel Edgewater managed to get a supply in before the government stopped supporting the troops. We're probably good on that count."

"That's good to know," Joe said.

"Guess I better be getting back out front," Edna said. She started to turn, hesitated, then said, "I ever tell you how much I appreciate you, Joe?"

"Once or twice," he said with a smile.

"Well, let me tell you again. If it wasn't for all your years of dedicated hard work, I wouldn't have made a go of this place."

"That's not true," Joe said, "and don't let me hear another word about it."

"Okay, not another word, but just make sure you know how I feel."

She left it at that and returned to the front of the diner. A couple of customers were coming through the door. New faces in town. Wanda something-or-other, that sweet flower child whose name slipped her mind, and a nice young man named Bobby. They waved to her and took a table near the front of the diner.

Edna was getting used to new faces these days, with that handsome preacher man Jim Pierce and little Billy Evans being the most recent. Under better circumstances, they would have all been welcome additions to Faith.

Edna made her way over to where Billy was halfway through a tall glass of milk and licking the remains of blueberry pie from his plate.

"You getting enough to eat?" she asked.

"Boy's eatin' fine," Jed said.

"Yes, ma'am, I am," Billy said. "I sure like your pie."

"I'm glad you do."

The world could fall to pieces, but a good slice of pie would always be a comfort. That was something that could be counted on.

TWENTY-ONE

Edgewater slept fitfully. He dreamed of running through a storm of shambling dead things, plowing them down with an M-16 in one hand and his .45 in the other. He also dreamed of the bite, which he'd told no one about. He kept it hidden for now, until he'd done all the good he could do. Once word got out, they'd do to him what he'd do to any one of them.

Truth be told, he'd thought about doing himself, but the chemical reaction was already gaining control. Anything he could have done to prevent the inevitable should have been done a long time before now.

Edgewater sat up, staring at the oozing pus-filled wound on his arm. The shit coming out of it was black. His hands were shaking. It was all over for him now. Everything but the brain smorgasbord.

He found a pen and paper and scribbled a note on it. The note contained a short explanation and an address. Dalton would know what to do with it. He sealed the note in an official military envelope and wrote DALTON CONNORS across the front of it.

The sun would be coming up soon. Edgewater dressed in full combat gear and left his warm bed behind to walk down the center of Main Street. Beads of sweat ran down his face, but his skin was clammy cold, just like the skin of any corpse. If he'd had the balls to look in the mirror before taking to the streets, he'd have seen the grayish-white thing looking back, already beginning the stages of decay that would make him one of them.

He passed Edna's place, where he knew Edna and Joe would be right now, getting ready to open up and feed the masses. He would never eat there again, so he continued on, stopping at the Sheriff's office long enough to slide the envelope addressed to Dalton under the door.

It was the last good thing he ever did.

By the time he reached the barrier separating Faith from the rest of the world, Edgewater was barely human. He passed a soldier coming off guard duty. When the soldier saluted and said, "Morning, Colonel Edgewater," the thing that used to be Edgewater didn't respond.

He let himself out of the wall and into the zombie wasteland beyond, crossing the stretch of highway separating Faith from the ridge to the east—the very ridge he'd led an assault against on more than one occasion.

A soldier on guard duty in one of the four towers that formed the corners of the Faith barricade couldn't believe what he was seeing. He grabbed the radio mic and keyed it. "Post two, do you copy?" he said.

There was a short burst of static, then a voice came over the channel. "Post two, go ahead."

The soldier on post one keyed his mic again. "I've got Colonel Edgewater in my sight right now. He's outside the barrier and heading for the ridge."

"Copy that," the soldier on post two responded. "I got an eyeball on him now. What the hell is he doing out there?"

"You tell me," the soldier one responded. "We need to—oh shit, what's he doing?"

Edgewater had fallen to his knees, now he was in the middle of a coughing fit. His muscles rippled and began to pulse and swell, expanding until his shirt ripped down the back and his M-16 fell away.

Edgewater screamed; his scream became a roar that shattered the still morning air and built to a crescendo that shook the ground.

The thing that was Edgewater rose to his feet, the rest of his clothes tearing and falling away like a snake shedding skin. His arms, legs, and chest expanded as he underwent a metamorphosis that turned him into a hulking beast. In the

95

distance, a horde of the walking dead rose over the top of the ridge to answer the call of their leader.

Edgewater raised his arms high and wide, welcoming them as they came down the side of the mountain toward him, descending on Faith in numbers larger than ever before.

"Sound the warning siren," the soldier on post two said. "Something's about to go down and it's not going to be good."

TWENTY-TWO

Dalton and Abigail were startled awake by the blaring scream of emergency sirens. They were used to the sirens, which always accompanied an attack. They had no idea this time would be different.

"Another attack," Dalton said, swinging his legs over the side of the bed and reaching for his pants. "You stay here."

"I'm going with you," Abby insisted.

He wanted to tell her no, but one look in her eyes told him it would be pointless. She was stubborn. Her mind was made up.

* * *

Colbrook and Sarah were together in the squad car. They'd been on their way to work when the siren sounded. Now they were speeding along Main Street, with Colbrook doing his best to avoid hitting the soldiers scrambling from makeshift barracks, some of them still half naked. In the process, a military truck pulled out in front of the speeding squad car. Colbrook swerved to avoid it. Doing so put him on a collision course with a tank. He slammed on the brakes, narrowly avoiding a head-on collision.

* * *

Johnny and Wanda met Bobby and Terri Lynn in the living room of the house the four of them were sharing. Johnny was already loading a shotgun.

"Another round of zombie hunt, kids,"

Bobby and Terri Lynn, who'd gotten accustomed to guns since coming to Faith, were grabbing weapons from the closet. Terri Lynn tossed a .44 Magnum to Wanda, who caught it, checked the rounds, and said, "Let's go."

* * *

The sky over Faith was pink and purple hued as the sun rose. U.S. fighter jets roared overhead. Joe and Edna stood outside the cafe, looking up at the jets as they flew overhead and circled back.

"Thank God they're not abandoning us," Edna said.

"It's about time we get some reinforcements," Joe added.

* * *

"What's happening?" Billy asked, rubbing sleep from his eyes as he followed Jed and Jim to the porch.

"That's the siren that tells us we're being attacked," Jed said. "Gonna get my rifle and join the troops." He pointed to the jets overhead. "Looks like we might have some help this time around."

"I'm coming too," Jim said.

"Count me in," Billy added.

"You stay here," Jim said.

"I have my own shotgun," Billy argued. "I took care of myself before you found me. I don't wanna sit here without doin' my share."

Jim was about to object again. Jed laid a hand on his arm. "Let the boy make his own mind up," he said. "It's a different world we're livin' in."

Jim looked at Jed, then to Billy, and said, "All right, you come along, but you stay close, understand?"

"I understand," Billy said.

"Now that that's settled, let's go kills us some zombies," Jed said.

* * *

"Jets, Dalton," Abigail said, clapping her hands in excitement. "We're going to be okay, aren't we?"

"Maybe so," he said, but there was a feeling in his gut that he couldn't shake. Air force jets flying overhead when Edgewater had made it clear the military was out of it didn't make sense to him.

Abigail was too happy to detect Dalton's lack of enthusiasm, and he wasn't about to bring her down. If there was even a little hope for them, he meant to let her enjoy every bit of it.

98

"I don't like it," Colbrook said.

"It's good, right?" Sarah said. "I mean, it's the military."

"I don't like the formation. It looks like we might be part of the target."

"Part of the target? That's insane. Why would they do that?"

"Maybe there's something here they don't want to risk losing," Colbrook said. "Maybe they've got a mistake to correct."

"You think they'd kill us all to do that?"

"I don't doubt it for a second," he said, checking the chamber in his gun. "Not for a single second."

* * *

Senior Airman Hensley keyed his mic. He'd flown missions in three combat zones, but never in his career had he seen anything like this.

"Colonel Edgewater is the Alpha Male," he said into the mic. "Confirm, Edgewater *is* the Alpha Male."

"What is his position?" a voice came back over the radio.

"Target is converging on Faith," Hensley said, "and he's got a whole bunch of the dead with him."

"Are you prepared to engage?" the radio voice asked.

"Mission is a go," Hensley said.

"There will be casualties—"

"Roger that, mission is still a go," Hensley said.

"Then engage at will," the voice on the radio responded.

* * *

What appeared to be a sea of dead flesh moved toward Faith, with more coming over the ridge. Hundreds had already reached the Faith barricade, with Edgewater in the lead. He'd become a hulk of a creature, towering over his minions, his blood red and his veins pulsating and squirming as the virus fed on itself in his veins.

Edgewater tore through Faith's barricade, tossing the heavy wood aside as if he were ripping apart a craft stick project. He stormed straight into town, overturning a truck full of soldiers in his path.

The horde rushed in behind him and fanned out. The zombies in front took the bullets while others spilled past them and overwhelmed the soldiers by sheer numbers.

Soldiers screamed as the dead swarmed over them, ripping limbs from their bodies and feasting on flesh. There were so many of the dead that the living didn't stand a chance. Many of them turned their weapons on themselves, preferring to blow their brains out than to end up rising again.

The first wave of firebombs slammed into Faith, spreading flames that engulfed zombies and soldiers alike. The screams of human suffering and banshee wails of the walking dead collided, along with sporadic bursts of gunfire and the roar of flames, until it was impossible to distinguish the sounds from one another.

For several minutes flame and thick smoke prevented the fighter pilots from assessing damage. When the smoke cleared, they saw Edgewater was still on the move, barreling through the men he'd once commanded. He was lifting them like rag dolls, snapping their spines, and tossing them aside like garbage.

"Target is not down," Hensley said. "I repeat, target is not down. We're going in again."

The jets came in for another round, incinerating more of the walking dead. Edgewater flipped a jeep onto its side just as the missiles found their targets. Flames engulfed the vicinity and spread out. The afterblast flattened buildings on all sides of the target zone. It looked from the air like this round was successful, then Edgewater emerged from a wall of flame, his skin bubbling, and charged after a group of soldiers trying to make their way to the safety of their trucks.

The soldiers, reeling from the knowledge that they'd been abandoned and sacrificed by their government, didn't realize Edgewater was coming. He tore through them, leaving a scattered trail of body parts in his wake.

Edgewater was ground zero for a third assault, and while this one tore him to shreds, a good portion of Faith went with him.

"They're blowin' up the whole fuckin' town," Johnny said.

He was trapped on the front porch with Wanda, Bobby, and Terri Lynn, surrounded by the infected dead. The four of them had fought like hell, but there was no getting around the horde.

"Inside," Johnny said, pushing Wanda toward the door. To Bobby and Terri Lynn, he said, "Go with her, both of you."

"What are you doing, Johnny?" Wanda demanded.

"Get inside," he barked, leaving no room for argument.

Wanda held his gaze for a moment, wanting more than anything to stop him from whatever he was planning.

"I gotta do this," he said. "Let me and my five-hundred dollar suit get to the top of that ladder, okay?"

How could she argue with that? Johnny Boscoe wanted to make it to the big time. This was his ticket.

She kissed him and turned away, following Bobby and Terri Lynn inside.

Johnny looked after her until the door closed, then he faced the horde.

"Lock and load," he said.

He jumped from the porch and forced his way through the rotten motherfuckers, drawing as many as he could away from the house. He emptied his shotgun, then he used it like a baseball bat, mowing down anything that got in front of him.

"Son of a bitches," he yelled, angling toward the main skirmish at the front barrier of town.

The help he expected there wasn't forthcoming. A few soldiers opened fire, but they were quickly overwhelmed.

Johnny fought until he went down too.

* * *

Edna and Joe fought side by side behind the counter that had served an endless parade of customers, particularly this past week. The infected came in the front and back doors, Deputies Johnson and Walker among them, maybe drawn to the diner by some deep-seated memory.

There was no time for a cup of coffee or homemade pie this morning. There was only Edna and Joe, each with a pistol and limited ammunition, and they served up hot lead the same way they'd always served up food, with smiles on their faces.

They died with dignity, while just outside the diner, Deputies Hagerman and Swanson went down the same way, firing their weapons until they were out of ammunition and could fight no more.

* * *

"Get in the car," Colbrook said to Sarah.

He climbed in behind the wheel and backed away from the fire zone, not even bothering to turn the car around until he was at the end of the street, then he glanced at the burning wasteland in his rearview mirror. He slammed on the brakes and pounded a fist against the steering wheel.

"I'm going back," he said. "I can't just run away and leave everybody dying behind me. I want you to drive as far away from here as you can."

"Jeff, no . . ."

"*Go*, Sarah. Get the hell away from here. If I think you're safe, I'll do better, but if I think you're in the middle of this, I won't be able to concentrate. Do you understand that?"

She nodded.

He took the shotgun from its mount, grabbed ammunition from the glove box, and leaned over to kiss Sarah, then he got out and headed back to the war zone on foot.

* * *

"Come on, you dead sons of bitches," Jed said, raising his rifle to pick another one of the zombies off with a clean head shot.

Jim was right behind him, shoving a fresh clip into his Uzi. Right beside Jim, now carrying a handgun (at Jim's insistence), was Billy. The three of them advanced on the zombies, made a stand, then advanced some more.

"I'm too damn old to let a bunch of smelly cadavers get the best of me," Jed said. "I ain't goin' down without a fight."

"I hear you," Jim said.

He opened fire and sprayed a corpse in camouflage. The line of bullets cut across the zombie soldier's chest, tearing through a name tag that read Pvt. Hawkins. Before the dead soldier could come at him again, Jim brought his Uzi up and let loose with a burst that took Pvt. Hawkins' head right off.

Billy handled his new weapon like a skilled marksman. He felt more comfortable with the pistol and liked that it didn't knock him on his butt whenever he pulled the trigger.

Jed raised his rifle as a corpse lurched in front of him. The thing was too damn close and the barrel of the rifle deflected, throwing Jed off balance. He was in the process of trying to get his rifle up again when the lumbering thing hit him hard, knocking him backward. He did a good job keeping his balance until his heel caught on one of the fallen corpses, then Jed went down on his ass so hard the wind left him in one fell swoop.

Jim spun toward Jed and the zombie, bringing his Uzi into firing position. The Uzi stuttered for just a second before the clip was empty, leaving the zombie over Jed still in one piece.

"Shit," Jim said, fumbling for another clip.

Billy's handgun exploded. The bullet tore through the back of the zombie's head. The zombie stiffened, then toppled over Jed, who looked up at the boy with admiration.

Jim was just about to slam a fresh clip into his Uzi when he was attacked from behind. Billy turned in time to see it, but there was nothing he could do. One of the things bit into Jim's neck, tearing out his jugular. Others crowded around, and after a few seconds, Jim's screams were lost in the steady buzzing and slurping sounds of feeding zombies.

* * *

A newscast was playing somewhere in the background.

Wanda watched two soldiers carry away Johnny's remains. There wasn't much there, but she insisted on looking at what was left.

Bobby and Terri Lynn stood by for support.

". . . after worldwide strikes against the infected, the President of the United States has declared that the situation is under control . . ."

Dalton, Abigail, Colbrook, and Sarah moved among the wounded, doing what they could to help out. Occasional gunshots reminded them that not every survivor was coming out of this alive.

The newscast continued.

". . . While it will be some time before we experience complete recovery, we can rest assured the worst is behind us and we are on the road to recovery, not only as a nation, but as a planet. . . ."

The smoldering remains of Faith were the same as the smoldering remains of towns across the state of Wyoming. Those smoldering towns were the same as smoldering towns and cities across the United States, which in turn mirrored the smoldering remains of towns and cities worldwide. It would be a long time before the planet recovered. . . .

* * *

ONE YEAR LATER

Dalton poured a cup of coffee and headed for the porch. He stopped and looked into the bedroom, where Abigail lay sleeping with the early-morning sunlight in her hair. He stayed long enough to enjoy the sight of her, as he often did these days. It was a pleasure he would never deny himself.

It seemed a lifetime ago that the dead had risen. Edna's place was still where it had always been, surprisingly untouched by the final blistering attack on Faith. Abigail opened it every morning Monday through Saturday, never once forgetting Edna or Joe as she went about keeping the diner alive.

Jeff Colbrook (no longer Sheriff Colbrook because he'd given up the office) and Sarah lived on a small farm not far from Dalton and Abby's place. They'd taken up raising horses, which made the two of them happy.

Wanda, Bobby, and Terri Lynn opened a store in the rebuilt section of Faith. A candle and incense store. They didn't do a lot of business, but it was a living they enjoyed. Wanda became quite the country girl, often wondering what it would have been like had Johnny survived. She thought about him often, smiling when she imagined him living the country life.

Dalton still wrote paperback westerns, and Jed, along with Billy, who he'd unofficially adopted, still stopped by for the occasional beer and a signed copy of Dalton's latest book.

Dalton looked at Abigail a moment longer, then he went out to the porch and sat down to read Edgewater's journal. He'd retrieved it from a safe deposit box in Edgewater's hometown, which happened to be in South Dakota. Edgewater, it turned out, was a transplanted small-town boy.

Dalton had possessed the journal for a year now. He wasn't sure what to do with it. Edgewater had led him to it, so he thought maybe he was supposed to write it all down and give it to the public. The note Edgewater had written was simple: Do what you believe is right.

He opened the journal and began reading from the beginning. The first entry was dated one year before the meteorite struck Faith.

Edgewater's Journal Entry, January 2009:

They've known about it since 1970. I knew too, even though I was barely a teenager back then. My father, General Martin Edgewater, wrote it all down. He kept the papers in a safe in his study. I inherited those papers when he died in 1995. I wish to God I hadn't.

The black shit in those meteorites has been here before. Our government studied it and hid the findings away, hoping to never have to deal with it. Who could guess there'd be more?

I have Alpha Male Syndrome. Some people call it 47 XYY. It means I have one more male chromosome than most of the rest of the male population. 47 XYY effects one in every thousand men. It makes me the arrogant son of a bitch I am today.

What on God's green fucking planet does that have to do with anything? Let me tell you. The black shit in those meteorites has an effect on anyone it comes into contact with. Touch it, breathe it, hell, even look at it, it kills you and makes you walk again. Brings dead things out of the ground too. I pray to God we'll never have to see it in action.

The black shit has another effect on those with Alpha Male Syndrome. Anybody with 47 XYY that comes into contact with it

or gets bitten or scratched by someone infected with it ends up
an Alpha Male Corpse, leading hordes of the slathering dead like
some rotted messiah.

Our government recorded it. General Martin Edgewater kept
a copy of the tape. Colonel Clayton Edgewater, yours truly,
inherited that too. I won't talk about all the things our
government did on the tape, but suffice to say, it ain't fucking
pretty. The 47 XYY subject they experimented on became a
raging hulk who could only be brought down with a rocket
launcher. Where do you think they found that subject? They
didn't just happen on a corpse with 47 XYY. Somebody with the
extra chromosome had a " government accident."

A big, strong bastard with a bad attitude. That's what the
poor fucker became. I've always fancied myself a big, strong
bastard with a bad attitude, but not like it happens with the black
shit. That's not the way I want to be remembered. I'm a proud
American, and like me or not, I don't give a damn, I do what I do
for my country. I've always done what I do for my country.

I love my country.

If this ever comes to pass, understand that I will put a bullet
in my brain. I will not become a monster. I will not inflict on the
United States of America what I would become if the black shit
ever sees the light of day again and I am infected by it.

I will not lead an army of the dead.

Dalton closed the journal.

Abigail came up behind him and wrapped her arms around
him, leaning down to kiss him on the cheek. "Good morning,"
she said.

"Good morning."

He turned his head so he could kiss her lips.

"What are you deep in thought about?" she asked.

"I'm starting a new book," he said. "Something with a little
more punch than a western."

With that, he kissed Abby again, then headed for his
typewriter.

www.ingramcontent.com/pod-product-compliance
Lightning Source LLC
Chambersburg PA
CBHW071332130626
46556CB00004B/1859